The Visitors
& other stories & poems

Rowan Fortune-Wood
(editor)

Cinnamon Press
Independent Innovative International

Published by Cinnamon Press
Meirion House
Glan yr afon
Tanygrisiau
Blaenau Ffestiniog
Gwynedd LL41 3SU
www.cinnamonpress.com

The right of the contributors to be identified as the authors of this work has been asserted by them in accordance with the Copyright, Designs and Patent Act, 1988. © 2010
ISBN 978-1-907090-05-9
British Library Cataloguing in Publication Data. A CIP record for this book can be obtained from the British Library

Designed and typeset in Palatino & Garamond by Cinnamon Press
Cover design by Mike Fortune-Wood from original artwork:
'House' by Alexandr Tkachuk, supplied by agency: dreamstime.com

Introduction

The Visitors and Other Stories & Poems is the ninth Cinnamon Press competition anthology and unites a strong selection that displays the quality of contemporary writing. Like the previous two competition anthologies it has been a great privilege to publish and edit.

Two poets emerged as clear joint-winners, Anne Caldwell and Sally Douglas, although all the poetry here is demonstrative of the talent we had to pick from. Caldwell's piece 'Walk in the Park' exemplifies her subject matter and thematic concerns; from the first person voice of a baby on a life support machine we are given a retrospective contrast between the present environment, 'I'm kept in a box. I blink./ Smell hot plastic.' and the womb, 'I've lost her metronome heartbeat.' Visual details give a strong impression of the scene, 'Stretch out my hand/ to watch a pattern of light redden./ I'm a glow-in-the-dark; half-fish/ with slithery lungs in a ribcage supple as a slipper.' Douglas's poem 'Mute', the first in a sequence called 'Broken Air', uses repetition to create a sense of mounting insistence, addressing the second person perspective 'If you had done[…]', 'If this had happened[…]' Asserting, 'If what you say is true, there would be records,/ not poems.' and culminating with the final forcful stanza, 'But all you have done is create these things,/ opaque as swans.'

A sense of loss, searching and discovery pervades much of the prose; from Douglas Bruton's 'The Stories Fantastical of Noah McGonagall' and its titular character's boat, 'Perdu', to the liberating metaphysical transgression depicted in Marianne Jones's 'The Kiss'—both of which examine such themes with a cleverly humorous tone. These stories move from the sweeping narratives of a sympathetic character beset by events, as with Janet Swinney's 'Offerings and Thanksgivings', to strange introspective memories, as with Muhamed Fajkovic's 'Vivisection'. A feeling of melancholy and grief is frequently central. This is particularly true in Tricia Durdey's winning story 'The Visitors', in which this haunting aspect permeates the text. Durdey's writing has an accent of horror: a woman visited by a mother and child needing refuge, with so much merely hinted at. The reader is forced to be attentive to the nuances and ambiguities.

Rowan Fortune-Wood
Tŷ Meirion, April 2010

Contents

The Visitors
& other stories & poems

Sally Douglas

Creek

A low moon through the trees
and the tide's pulse inwards—
nets, rods, lines stowed neatly,
and a dark wake following.

Bumping the sludgy edge, the boat
shivers, lets the tide slide around it.
Empty branches fracture the sky.

And I think of those springs when
need was so strong that the road became river;
that pull of things, over and back,
like your slow breath sliding;
and the fish, gulping.

The moon is smeared over the river's skin,
like unction. I turn with the tide.

End of Term

('...Exeter St David's, Dawlish, Teignmouth, Newton Abbot...')

The train has always slowed here, at the edge.
Back then I'd be hoping for the water's fling and scour
against my twin-ghost image in the glass:
a baptism I didn't need to feel.

But now I watch the inland side,
where daily frictions strip
the past wide open.
I trace the hard-ribbed lines of sediment
to find the restless sand.

Where two things meet is where you feel things most.

Tonight I'll wade into the ocean.
The surface will be a bright cold wire
rising round me, upwards, up towards to my throat,
slicing through my body like a scan.

From 'Broken Air': A sequence

1. Mute

If you had done what you say you have done
you would have scars.

If this had happened as you say,
someone would have noticed.

If he had done this thing you say he has done,
you would have spoken then.

If what you say is true, there would be records,
not poems.

We have looked for records.
There are none.

If what you say is true, the dark would be spooling out
behind you.

But all you have done is create these things,
opaque as swans.

2. Inside

The breath of a wall
nothing but a shimmer of air on a hot road
nothing but a curtain of change between inside and out

Nothing but lips pressed together
not taped
not sewn but pressed
like hands in prayer

A hand against nothing can make a wall

You slide your fingertips over the cold nothing
open your mouth
the words come out
       frantic as birds against glass

3. Linden Tree

'Thence up he flew, and on the Tree of Life...
Sat like a Cormorant' (Paradise Lost: Milton)

Afterwards, she remembers feathers.
Feathers caped around her,
wings straitjacketing her arms
as if she might have struggled.

How she thought an angel was behind her
until that terrible pressure:
the black mask snaking over her shoulder
the flicker at her breast.

Oh, but the words
sliding over her—words dark as olives,
the unhearable words—
words slick as oil.

Afterwards she wants to clothe herself in feathers
feel the barbs, the pinions,
but all she has is leaves.

Wendy Holborow

When You Chance Upon

When you chance upon a herd of goats
with clinking bells
hooves chinking like china cups
on steep Greek mountain paths,
where the yellow poppy grows
transmuted from mellow Welsh meadows
to this harsh unrelenting space,
it isn't something you mention
because it's common place.

When you chance upon a field of asphodels
and instinct tells you what they are
because you've learned from the great Greek poets
and yearn to emulate the best
it isn't something you mention
unless to impress a guest

and when some skinny cats slink beside you
braving the dog to beg
for greasy chips
you know you're not in the soft Welsh hills
but the bald mountains of Greece
where the wind seizes breath
steals it like an Ondine curse
and the clunking of the goats' bells
swell the silence.

In The Presence of Madness

I would not call you mad
though your madsmile madness
gnaws at the awning of your
awareness and we realise
that you are living in isolation
in the isobubble
of your madmuddle mind.

You tap the side of your nose
in that Machiavellian way, as if you have
important secrets to hide.

It was me you came to last year
when you could no longer cope
were trembling the high
tightrope, stretched
ready to
        break.

You left a pitched wake in which
I thought I would drown, afraid
that you were dragging me into your
breakdown, into
your mad mildewed mind.

I sensed I was in
The Presence of Madness.

I kept away this time
asked friends politely
        how is he?
distanced, detached because
I did not want you to
leave me heaving on the shore
of the osmotically insane.

The Stories Fantastical of Noah McGonagall
Douglas Bruton

Noah McGonagall lost his wife. Fifty-two years in the same house, the same bed, and she went first, from this life to the next. Noah McGonagall, big as a bear and his arms hanging loose at his sides, his hands empty. Empty is what he would have said, reaching for Dilys' small hands, and finding nothing in his grasp except air.

Lost more than Dilys. That's the truth. That's what they said down at the post office. Lost all his reason, and maybe that was all it was. He kept all the lights on in his house and played the radio turned up loud. Neighbours looked the other way at first, marked the days off on their calendars, and waited for the madness to pass.

But the madness of Noah McGonagall was not quickly over.

'Wouldn't you feel the same if you'd lost a Dilys,' said Rachel McAllister one morning.

And the women that had gathered in Rachel McAllister's front room nodded in agreement, and after tea and shortbread biscuits, fantails not fingers, they made soup for Noah McGonagall. Miriam Black carried it to his door, hot and in cans with lids. She asked him if there was anything else she could do.

He tilted his head as if listening to birdsong or wind.

'Do you hear that?' said Noah McGonagall.

Maybe there were voices in his head. That's what Miriam Black thought. That's how she told it when she spoke of it to the other women. To Noah McGonagall she said, 'I don't hear nothing. There's nothing to be heard, I swear it.'

'And there should be something,' said Noah McGonagall. 'Don't you think there should be something?'

Miriam Black had no answer to that.

Then one day Noah McGonagall began to build the boat. Right there in his back garden, like he was the Noah out of the minister's book, all beard and staff and spoke to by God. Not so big as an ark, but no mistaking the hull of a boat taking shape, there on the grass, and all the noise of hammers and nails and saws and sanding through the long days.

Miriam Black brought lamb in a stew to his door. Or beef in

a pie. Sausages cooked in gravy. Pasties with potato and carrot and meat.

'A man needs a woman,' said Rachael McAllister. 'Otherwise he fades away.'

The women, over tea, agreed. So they baked bread, and cake, and bannocks, and scones.

'Rain is it you're expecting, Noah?' said Corey Scott. 'Is that why you is building a boat here, as far from the sea as a man can get? Rain is it?'

The driest summer on record. That's what they said on the radio. Noah McGonagall must have heard it too. Still he measured the wood, and cut it with the saw, and smoothed it with the plane, and fitted it to his boat.

Boys from the school stopped at the bottom of his garden and took to calling him names, and they laughed, and threw stones at mad Noah McGonagall. And girls laughed too and stuck their tongues out at him behind his back. And the parents of the children told them they shouldn't, not the laughing or the stones or the tongues, and they shook their heads and talked on corners about what Noah McGonagall was about.

'Is it a change in the weather you think? Is that what's coming?' said Corey Scott.

But it was as if Noah McGonagall was deaf. He didn't look up from his work, not once. The smell of tar and paint, oil and varnish hung in the thickening air. And the boat one day bore a name. Letters of gold painted on a black painted ribbon. 'Perdu'.

'That means lost,' said Miriam Black. 'It's French.'

'It's sad is what it is,' said Alice Gracey, and she dabbed at her eyes with her napkin, and drank her tea, and asked for a second cup if she could.

The laughter went away, and voices shrank to whispers, and every day a small gathering looked over his garden fence wondering at the boat 'Perdu' and what would happen when at last it was done.

Then came the day. Noah aboard his boat. Like a boat it was, with a sail and a tiller. But wheels it had too. Four. Two on each side. Great spoked cartwheels. And there was Noah McGonagall, face turned to the sky, lips moving, like he was praying. Only he wasn't. Not prayers. He was singing. It was Corey Scott heard it first. Quiet like he was further off, that's what Corey said, but definitely singing. He was thin as a stick, despite the cooking Miriam Black delivered to his door every day. Thin as a stick and eyes sunken and Noah McGonagall singing, there on the deck of his boat. Singing through the day and into the starry night.

The next morning Miriam Black found on her doorstep the fifteen books from Noah McGonagall's library and two ladles and a soap-dish. Rachael McAllister had the ceramic horse and the wooden angel, towels and several cups. Gilbert MacDonald was gifted a chest of tools and plates with tulips painted on the rims. Alice Gracey got two porcelain cats and a suitcase of dresses and a silver-backed mirror with roses on the handle. And Corey Scott now owned Noah McGonagall's radio and a tin kettle and a tea caddy with pink enamel flowers on a black enamel background. Everyone in the village had some part of Noah McGonagall.

It was known then. There was a feeling, in every man and woman and child: something was missing. Like something you had was suddenly taken from you, or just now noticing it lost. Even before they saw it was gone, they knew. There were the marks of wheels gouged into the grass of Noah McGonagall's garden, and the fence was down. The tracks led to the road. Then nothing. A space left behind where he once was.

A note pushed into a milkbottle on Noah McGonagall's front doorstep said 'no more deliveries, please'.

The women did not know what to say. Over tea and toasted crumpets they sat in silence in Janie Tallis' parlour, sat close to the window, looking over to where Noah McGonagall had been only the day before. Noah and his boat on wheels.

What was there to say now he was gone? At the post office they swapped good mornings and good days. But they did not feel good. In the street, they stopped to share a word and shared instead a sigh and then silence.

The men too, said little. Though they never said much before, the feeling was that something was well and truly lost in the losing of Noah McGonagall.

Then one day, Corey Scott was seen mending the fence in Noah McGonagall's garden, putting it back together and speaking to Noah as if he was there.

'Gone is it?' he said. 'Like on a journey? Like you had a plan all along.'

And maybe that was it. Not mad after all, but with a plan. Right from the start. From the first sawn piece of wood and the first nail and the first drawn diagram for his boat. And when Corey Scott returned the next day to tend the grass in Noah McGonagall's garden, he began to imagine that journey, came over all lyrical, and he told the boys on their way home from school, the ones that still stopped to wonder at the gap left behind by Noah McGonagall gone. And the girls too.

'I reckon he's gone to see an aunt of his.' Corey Scott leaning on his old lawn-mower, and telling a story. 'Far from here, he has gone. Sailing the fields, with a spyglass to one eye and one hand on the tiller. Calling 'ahoy' and 'hard about' and 'splice the mainsail'. Gulls following in his wake, probably, grey backed and herring, rising and falling like they's tied to the stern with string, like they's balloons or kites. And Noah McGonagall laughing at the bumps under his wheels, like the sea when it is choppy, and he steadies himself, finding his sea-legs, shifting his weight from one foot to the other, looking like he is dancing on the deck of his boat.'

Corey Scott imagining an aunt to visit. Passing the story on and Miriam Black telling her husband over dinner. 'Name of Millicent. Noah McGonagall's Aunt. Hair like silver and eyes sparking blue as the blue flames of my gas cooker. Well, one eye at least, for the other is hid under a black leather eye-patch. That's where he's gone. To an aunt. And with a following wind he'll be there soon, a day or two at most.'

Alice Gracey's husband, who never hears a word his wife says, has heard the story. He tells Alice. Lying side by side in the one bed, looking at the ceiling, not looking at each other. 'Millicent or Milli. An aunt on his mother's side. House on a hill and fish in glass bowls on every shelf and every table and in all the windows. Orange and blue and yellow, with tails like thin cloth and eyes that never sleep. And on the walls, maps of all the places there are in the world, and notes in the corners, looks like writing anyway, in some sort of code that only Millicent can read. Noah McGonagall gone to buy one of those maps. It is certain. Everyone's saying so.'

At school they had a competition to design Noah McGonagall's map, the one he paid for, with a gold coin he had sewn into the hem of his coat. A treasure map, or a map to a lost place. Bobby McAllister drew an island with a cigarette on

19

and a pound coin and a snail in a jar. He told the teacher that these are things he has lost and Noah McGonagall has gone to find all the lost things and to bring them back. The poetry in what Bobby McAllister said was a surprise to his teacher, Mrs Trowie.

Corey Scott set to painting the fence for the winter. His own fence first and then Noah McGonagall's. The same dark green. He pulled weeds from the flower borders and cut back the privet. Then he swept the cuttings into a heap. Stopped to catch his breath, leaning on the handle of the brush.

'Gone to the edge of the world,' he told the boys who were late for school. 'That's where he's gone. Just to see. To look over the edge and see what's there. Dragons there used to be. You see them on old maps, like the ones on aunt Millicent's walls. Dragons with their tails all coiled and scaly. That's where Noah McGonagall's gone.'

Miriam Black doesn't believe there's an edge to the world, not like there is for a plate, like you could look over it and see dragons or serpents. 'That's just what map makers did when the map they were drawing reached bits that they did not know,' she told Rose MacDonald. 'It's the edge of the known world is where Noah McGonagall has gone. That's what Corey Scott means. As far as far can be. Where the women dress in skirts made out of grass and eat blue fruit and the birds speak words and wear their feathers all bright as crayons.'

'What does he want there, then?' said Lillian Gurney at the shop, her hair still in curlers and no make-up on.

'What do all men want?' said Cathy Dell.

Corey Scott shovelled snow from the path in front of Noah McGonagall's house. Laid down salt, just like he'd done in front of his own house and in front of Rose MacDonald's.

'In search of unseen wonders, I should expect. See Venice and die, they say. Well, he's likely seen that in his travelling. Now he's off in search of what hasn't been seen. Don't ask me what that might be, because it ain't ever been seen, so how would I know?'

Corey was running out of ideas. Not just Corey.

'Temples in dark jungles, some of them hasn't been seen. There was a programme about it on the television,' said Miriam Black.

But that didn't make sense. Noah McGonagall's boat adrift

in a jungle somewhere. Nobody had anything to add. That might have been the end of it all. There and then. Except Christmas cards came through the doors of all the villagers. Every card the same, just the names different, all signed 'Noah McGonagall'.

'Probably on his way home as we speak,' said Gilbert MacDonald over a pint, and not his first. 'Bringing us presents from exotic places, I shouldn't wonder. Flowers made of glass and wind up mice that sing, and stones that taste of toffee, and hats that make you clever when you wear them and glasses that let you see the world all rosy and laughing.'

The stories started again and the poetry, too. Corey Scott seen planting potatoes in the turned soil in Noah McGonagall's garden that Spring. Treating the garden like his own. Got it looking nice. And telling stories again of a man called Noah and a boat on wheels and sailing to other places. The boys and the girls had lost interest, so Corey Scott was telling the stories to himself, mostly.

And the year unfolded, turned over and there were cards again, same as before, and like before all signed 'Noah McGonagall'.

Year upon year, Corey Scott saying over, 'Do you remember?' And soon they didn't and still he dug up potatoes from another man's garden and painted two fences instead of one and cut the grass in two places and shifted the snow from more than his own bit of path.

Till, one year the cards didn't come. Not that year or the year after. Nobody really noticed, it seemed. Leastways, nobody said anything. And if they remembered, they kept it all to themselves, the travels of mad Noah McGonagall.

One day, Corey Scott, not as young as he was, if he ever was, saw something from a dream. Rubbed his eyes and looked again, not believing what he saw. A boat made of wood and nails and a sail raised and four cartwheels turning. Coming up the street, coming to rest outside the house that was empty. At the helm a man with a beard that Corey Scott recognised, even after all these years. By his side a woman, small as small, her hand in his.

'Is it away you've been, Noah?' said Corey Scott.

The woman laughed. 'Seeing the world, maybe?'

Noah McGonagall did not answer. He folded the mainsail

away, tied the boat to the gatepost of his house and helped the woman down.

'She's a little unsteady on her feet, or maybe it's dancing she is.' That's what Corey Scott told Miriam Black and Rachael McAllister. 'And you'll never guess,' he said.

'They'll be tired from their journey,' the women decided, so they made bread and scones and cakes and marched in a line up the path to Noah McGonagall's house, Miriam Black at the front.

'And is there anything else we can do?' they asked Noah McGonagall. Because they could see it was him.

He tilted his head as if he was listening to birdsong or the wind.

'Do you hear that?' said Noah McGonagall. There was singing at his back. A woman's voice. They could all hear that.

'Her name's Dilys,' he said. 'Now, isn't that the strangest thing.' And he winked when he said it so that they did not know if he spoke the truth. And he laughed, too.

There were no words at first from the women in front of Noah McGonagall's house. As they departed, they noticed a new name painted in gold letters on a painted black ribbon on the side of the boat.

'Trouvée,' said Miriam Black. 'That's French. It means found.'

Sue Moules

The Moth Box

We have caught the night,
it sleeps in here,
pulled in by light.

We open it in day,
take out the shapes
and name them.

Scorched Wing, Tussock,
White Ermin, Marbled Coronet,
Green carpet, Phoenix.

We lift them out,
look at them through hand lenses.
marvel at their intricacy.

We leave them in the shade
to sleep out,
they merge into garden.

Later they will flap in quick quivers,
heat their delicate tiled wings
fly into the dark.

Martin Willitts Jr

Divinization

In Norse mythology, Odin hung himself on an ash tree for nine days to learn the runes.

I have cut some branches
from the only fruit bearing tree in the ice forest
and curved on its spines the secret meanings known only to me.
A secret well kept is like a sharp two-headed axe.
A man that can hold his own breathe in his hands in the winter
can always find the source of the sun frozen in the sky.

I scattered these fragments of scrawled branches onto a white cloth,
white as the forever landscape,
white as my beard when ice forms on it edge.
A secret shared brings new enemies.
A man should do everything to keep to himself
when he cannot see anything.

I closed my frostbit eyes for a moment before lifting my head
and staring into the face of the frost gods.
Now I can interpret these three pieces of wood
like it was a woman under white skins and calling me to come.
A secret whispered into a woman's ear always causes laughter
like the tingle of icicles. A man can only hold so many things.

I can see the clear path in front of me, even in this endless darkness.
A secret is a world of snow devouring your footsteps
so no one can follow. A man who keeps things simple and familiar
will always be able to read runes. For each rune casting
and each interpretation is as individual as each man.

Canadian Geese

The noisy beginnings, the leaving stretching the sky,
the interminable returns,

they come & depart in an right angle taking the treetops off
as a wedge into a last echoed song,

this ritual happens twice yearly, never the same, never
changing, always knowing when the change is coming

they announce this change, breaking the icy clouds,
like laying eggs, like hatchlings breaking free in taps & cracks,

they remember what we forget:
things are the same & different, always in flight, always nesting,

we cannot lift out of our bodies, nor see the land slowly below us,
nor call the changing of the seasons so it will change like they can,

this is how love begins, the calling & responding,
this is how we should migrate & mate, and dip into water,

taking turns leading & following so neither tires,
in a formation of co-operation so none are left behind

Mary Robinson

Migrant

There are places
                that call us each year—

the valley held taut
              by the mountains

with no issue
          but the sea

where the sand
            shimmers with mica

and we tread
          the old track to the village

catching
      the background rasp

of insects
        in the reeds,

a pair of geese
          backlit against the water,

and I realise
        that what we hear,

as the marsh marigolds
            fix the faltering

sun's last light,
         are not insects at all,

but grasshopper
         warblers reeling,

and I wonder
        if you will ever

return.

Captain Cook's dinner service

Each evening, as the sky bloomed with stars,
dinner was served.
Red roses on white china
plates rimmed with gold, the edges crimped
into }s—bringing together
Resolution and *Discovery*,
skirting the continent's shore,
the fractured ice by day,
by night the aurora's emerald and ruby.

It was not meant to end like this—
two ships putting into Stromness
with their cargo of grief and loss.
I could smell peat smoke
as we entered the harbour,
fish curing and late haymaking.
Linen was drying on sandstone walls
and high up a skein of geese
sailed across the sky.

Jetsam or salvage? I gave them away—
those bowls, ice cracked, dirt glued.
They kept too many memories—
blood and bone gilded with sand,
our captain's grave on a Hawaiian shore.
Now, where the slope of the hill hides
the ocean, they sleep,
safe in a glass case in the House of Skaill.

The Kiss
Marianne Jones

Jesus had brown hair, sad eyes and a white robe down to his ankles. On this robe, he wore his heart with a golden cross over it. He was good and I loved him but he gave us red and blue books of sins called catechisms. The red was a basic book and the blue was advanced and told you about the Ten Commandments and seven deadlies in detail. When our priest, Father O'Maley, taught us from these books, he raised his voice as if he were telling a horror story, which indeed he was with all that talk of hell and damnation and eternal torment. One fine spring morning, he described the fire and stench of hell to us as he was standing near a bowl of lilies placed beside the altar for Easter. After that I had nightmares for three years and couldn't step on the fourth and fifth steps of our staircase because there were four letters in hell and five in devil. That's why I fell downstairs one night and bumped my hip and my head.

Father O'Maley could talk about any sin at great length but not the one in the sixth commandment. When I asked, 'What does 'Thou shalt not commit adultery' mean, Father?' he went silent and scarlet. It must be dreadful. Worse than murder.

'Kissing—is—wrong,' he spluttered in explanation. 'Not the way you kiss your parents, of course.'

'Uh! Kissing is for sissies,' the blue-eyed, spike-haired boy from Talafon estate said.

We laughed too loudly in our embarrassment and, after that, no one dared ask any more questions.

One May afternoon after school, when the wind was rolling dustbin lids down the hill, we were in catechism class when Father O'Maley said, 'Beware the world, the devil and the flesh.'

'But, Father, the sea and the world are beautiful,' I said, and thought of puddles to splash in later and the bluebells in my beloved dingle.

'Ah, yes, child. Indeed. But that's not what is meant by world.'

'What does it mean, Father?' I asked. And what did flesh mean? All I could think of were the legs of lamb and hams hanging up in Pritchard the butcher's window. Were my legs flesh as well? I pinched the skin on them and decided that there was definitely flesh in there. Beware the flesh!

'We don't have to go into all that now,' Father O'Maley said, making the sign of the cross over us in a hurry. 'Let us pray!'

We all fell to our knees. This gave the spike-haired boy a chance to whisper, 'Marbles?' to another boy.

'*O my God, I am heartily sorry for having offended Thee,*' Father O'Maley began.

'Behind the church?'

I worried the idea of the world as evil this way and that, but, in the end, decided that although I could not understand the idea, I would never sin again if I could help it. I would love Jesus until I died and would not stick any more nails into his crucifix.

William Williams had dusty blond hair and green eyes and, one day, my sister and I tied him up to a pine tree and went off for our lunch. It was on one of those June days when the fields are a sea of buttercups and lady's smock and the sun is like a bobbing boat in a foam of clouds and we were in the field behind our house and next to a disused school.

He hardly struggled at all. He wasn't even angry and, when I tied the last knot and looked up at him, he smiled straight into my eyes. Stunned, I followed my sister towards our house and climbed over the wall into our garden. Everything, except the colour of snapdragons and scent of mock orange, was a blur.

'Wash your hands,' my mother said as we reached the kitchen.

We did so with cracked carbolic soap and dinner was doled out. I stared at the massed clouds of mashed potatoes on my plate, and the smallholding of peas and stew. We all began to tuck in.

'So what have you two been up to this morning?' my father asked in kindly child-interrogation mode.

I cleared my throat violently, trying to use it as a signal to my sister to keep quiet, but it was too late.

'We tied a boy to a tree, Daddy,' she said, with a little smile.

There was silence and then my father bellowed, 'What?'

My sister froze like a shot rabbit. I felt sorry for her and was about to intervene when she started quailing, 'It was her idea, Daddy. It was her!' and pointed straight at me.

'What?' my father shouted at me. 'You tie a boy up to a tree and sit here eating your dinner! And how is he supposed to eat?'

I started wondering if I should take William Williams a slice of bread and cheese—after finishing my own lunch, of course.

'It's just a silly story, I'm sure,' I heard my mother say, but my father was on his feet and off to rescue William Williams from starvation. After a moment, he came back and yelled, 'Which tree?'

'Pine,' I said.

'Those straight behind the house?'

I nodded. My father stormed out.

'I'll go with him,' I said.

'You will not!' my mother said.

'But I know which one.'

'You will not, I said! I've spent hours slaving over a hot stove and you'll eat up. You're always up to something. What sort of example is that to your sister?'

My sister smiled coyly and I glared at her until I remembered that anger was one of the deadlies and turned my scowl into a wrenched smile.

My father came thundering back into the house. 'What the devil do you mean wasting my time like this?' he said. 'There's no one tied to a tree.'

'Oh!' I said and choked on my potatoes.

'You'd better stop making up these stupid stories of yours!'

'Eat up!' my mother said. 'And let's have no more of your foolishness. Father O'Maley is calling to see us at teatime and he's not going to be impressed by such nonsense.'

'You won't tell him?'

'That depends on how good you are.'

I sat up straighter but it was murder to have to finish my dinner without 'shovelling the peas into my mouth', and even worse drying the dishes afterwards while my sister dabbled her fingers in the soapy water and washed them with the speed of a tortoise.

'Hurry up!' I said.

My sister looked up at me from eyes beginning to enlarge with tears and called out, 'Mummy!'

'O.K.,' I said, trying to look patient.

A soapy plate was handed to me grudgingly. I polished it off quickly and waited like a dog who wants a stick thrown again. I shifted from foot to foot and craned my neck trying to see the

31

pine trees over the wall. I saw the top of one, blue-green and swaying in the wind. I snatched the next plate. An eternity later, we got down to serving dishes, ovenware, knives, forks, spoons.

As soon as we finished, I tore out of the kitchen and scrambled over the wall into the field. William Williams was indeed gone. I stared at the vacant tree. The rope was still there, attached at a higher level but free at one end.

My sister followed me over the wall.

'How did he untie all those knots?' she asked. 'It's like a miracle.'

'Don't know,' I said, swallowing my disappointment.

I was staring at the tree, when William Williams ran into the field like the Resurrection, caught hold of the end of the rope, and started swinging wildly to and fro singing *Mambo Italiana*. He looked so striking with his lack of fear, strength, hair glistening in the sunshine, that I just stood there watching him. I didn't notice that other boys had come into the field and were weaselling their way towards me, until one of them said, 'Shall we tie her up, Wil?'

My sister ran for our wall and hurried over it.

'Give her a dose of her own medicine, *te*?' another boy said.

They were beginning to surround me and I was pretending to be brave when William Williams dropped to the ground. 'Come on, *hogia*. Leave her alone,' he said.

'What, Wil, are you sure?' The boys moved closer to me.

'Come on, now,' William Williams said, striding into the middle of the ring that was forming around me. 'Leave her alone—let's go for a swim in the dingle.'

'You're not soft on her, are you?'

'Come on!'

The gang shuffled off in the direction of the dingle. Wil threw a smile over his shoulder at me just before he left the field through the old school gate. I stood there, staring after him. When I came back to my senses, the afternoon seemed cloudier and dull. My sister popped her head above the wall and one or two girls came to join us. We played tick and the group got bigger. There was a lot of sprinting about, which I loved, but something was missing. We changed the game to 'Hide and Seek' but that was boring too until I found a way into one of the school sheds on the field and climbed a rickety ladder into its loft to hide. There was one dusty skylight above me and in the half-darkness I made out the shape of boxes. My eyes got used to the low light and I went to explore: cardboard, light but full of something. I opened one of the boxes to find swords, shields and tinsel armour. They glistened in the gloom. There were two crowns as well, with gems made from coloured paper, and curtain cloaks. I was lost in a drama in which I figured as a princess and then a knight. The knight's life was more exciting and I invented a palomino called Pegasus for my adventures. These were interrupted by voices calling for me. I climbed down the ladder and out into the fresh air.

'We were looking for you everywhere!' my sister said.

'Come and see what's in here!'

But the girls were leaving, one after another, for their tea and my sister went to see if there were any Penguin biscuits on the table.

'I'll just fetch the rope,' I said, walking towards the tree. I looked up into its branches and then began to yank at the rope. The knots that fastened it tight were well above my reach.

'Can I help?' a voice behind me said.

It was Wil, his hair wet from swimming. He sauntered up to the tree and started to climb. He had the rope down in no time. Back on the ground, he said. 'I hope you didn't mind me swinging on it before. It seemed fair after being tied up!'

'Yes,' I said and cleared my throat. He held my glance. 'I'm sorry,' I said.

'No, it was quite funny,' he said.

'Oh!' He's so kind, I thought. 'How did you get free?'

'My friends came by - almost the moment after you left me to it.'

'Ah!'

There was an awkward pause.

'Run away with me!' he said.

'What?'

'Run away with me! We can run away from home together.'

I was thinking more about sprinting than leaving home but my adventures as a knight and something about Wil's gaze put me in high spirits and I was not in a hurry to return to the house. My Dad was still angry. I wanted to keep out of his way.

Wil caught hold of my hand and we started to walk, then run, towards the far end of the field. We raced faster and faster and there was a jumble of meadow, foxgloves, hedges, distant mountains, excitement and bewilderment in my head as we climbed over a hedge into another field. We raced on, past the smallholding where the farmer chewed tobacco and spat it out, through the field where I got chased by a bull and over a stile. We found ourselves enclosed in a small meadow with tall hedges. We stood there, out of breath and smiling at one another.

'Kiss me,' Wil said.

I looked up at him, startled and scared.

'I don't bite,' he said. 'Only a kiss. I promise.'

He took a step closer to me. The world span round. Father Maher's tea, the sixth commandment, the seven deadlies, and Jesus in his white robe span with it. Jesus! How could I give Him up for another man?

Wil touched my shoulder. 'Will you?' he asked, and then he kissed me.

Aisling Tempany

Tradition

The first thing I did when I got to Dublin
was have breakfast in the Kylemore Cafe
because it was our tradition.
We always had breakfast there.

You might like to know that
the cafe has been redecorated,
With plush red seats and a sleek new sign.
(But it still has a revolving door.)

I went to the Peace Garden
and the Hugh Lane too,
just like we'd always done.
The Nazi-wolf statue is gone

but there's an extension upstairs
with an abstract dying swan.
You would have liked that.
You would like that swan.

The LUAS tram is new though.
I went on it without you
From Connolly to Heuston station,
and walked to Kilmainham.

Where for the first time in years
I thought that I actually missed you.

Five of Us, Together

It was the five of us, together,
I thought that it would be forever.

But there was a day in November,
a rainy Saturday, where you packed
a bag and left,

and I begged to go with you
so at the door you stopped and waited,
while I packed a bag of my own.

There it was then, the two of us
walking along Blackpool promenade,
making a plan for the future.

Staying in bed and breakfasts,
buying new clothes and shoes,
going out by the sea.

Except it didn't last,
and you got tired of the rain
so you went back home instead.

The three of them said nothing
as I unpacked my bags,
but they said they liked my shoes.

We were all five back together
but I knew it was not forever.

Prydferth

You wrote it on a piece of paper
and passed it to me across the desk.
Did you think I understood it?
Did you think I would even care?

I had to go look it up in the dictionary
because my Welsh was far behind yours.
By the time I found the word in my book.
You'd already left the room sulking.

The dictionary said it meant *beautiful*.
I didn't write you anything back.

Noel Williams

Snow on the Edge

Erased the page of landscape waits.
Old childhoods have turned each gaunt thorn
and every scar of ditch and savage edge
to anticipation.
Winter skulls overnight grow lips and brows.
Clouds sleep. The road is lost. Hills inhale.

Our breaths meld in a single thought,
that the trail here and the ossuary under the snow
and the soft fist of earth battering the sky
have that same thought:
we all breathe each other here by our thinking.

The moment stands and stares at us, two figures
on a snowscape on a moor,
first marks in a sentence.

Return to High Force

Stretched out with your Kodak you lean beyond the brink
as if gravity's keener over the fall, poised, tilted to dive.
In that furious sluice you could relapse
for a few free moments of steep unearthly drop
that might elide the torrent in your head
into the hurl and mercy of the cascade.

Instead you toss down, one by one, her phrases
cold as farthings, nothing coins now,
spinning into white noise until you can't tell
if they're the glint of birds sniping or hooked fish—
or deceits from that voice beguiling as candlelight,
that voice whose whisper won't drown.

You're on your own. Down to the pool.
Desire ebbs here to quiet,
sidling through bracken laced by the shawl of spray.
Somehow the shout and hooligan of adolescent water
becomes puzzled by the trees, browses now
shyly, sliding by half-fallen pine, dark under skirts of larch.

Half-hid, wrapped over rocks wrecked in the Pleistocene
a silhouette stares across the water,
long fingers drawling through the wet, a kelpie draped in shadow.
That's when you recall the camera still wedged above the falls,
if not yet nicked with all it holds. The figure shifts,
ripples turning from the lazy hand, as if to speak,
as if you might find a new voice.

David Batten

Collwyd Yn Ffrainc, Mai 15 1917

... ac ni chaed ef, am ddarfod i Dduw ei symud ef ...
... and he was not found there because God had moved him from there ...

John Griffiths—
man of Harlech
annwyl fab, dear son
of Robert ac Elen
private yn y R.W.F.—
has a headstone
that looks over
the Norman ruins
of Castell Harlech
and Cricieth
and down
on the soft mounds
of the Llyn reaching out
for its Celtic twin

a headstone
but no bones
for John Griffith's bones
were lost in France

Embarkation

Despite a backlit sunset sky
a great moon hanging over France
ferry islands of light between smouldering shores
like banks of swept coals
a cruise ship at anchor strung and dripping with lights
floodlit Dover Castle
the red warning light on the antenna on the cliff
the White Cliffs themselves sub-shining
it's always gloomy when we cast off—
the soft chantings of Hail Marys and last rites
reaching me from much darker sailings.

Etaples

eat apples to Tommy
twelve thousand British and Commonwealth dead
immortalised under Lutyens arches
the dead not going away

this land—
this impeccable land tended with care
this tender square—
this land donated...
green

few chiselled words
name   rank   age
date of death
facts, where known
known unto god

not much left to say

eat apples

Marcus Smith

Famadihana (The Turning of Our Father)

Finally the dream arrived—
I heard you complain
you were cold in your tomb,
cold in ground that felt no sun.

We chose a hot May day,
my six brothers and I.
You, decayed nine years,
a shriveled log of bones and dust,
had roots sprouting from your skull.
Roots! we shouted with joy.

We dressed you in silk that cost me
six month's pay and my radio.
The turning-of band played
clarinet, drums and a dented tuba.
We held you high and danced
you through the whole village:

Here are your grandchildren
running barefoot over our dusty streets,
where hissing snakes still chase rats.
Here are the shanty clinic ruined by rains
and the charred schoolhouse
struck by lightning in the same storm.

Now you know,
just as your ancestors knew.
Bless us, father. Do what you can.

Driving Around

One thing I know about us,
we keep noticing them—

they fly over walls,
fly beyond everything
we have made.

See them circle the roads
mad with traffic,
ruled with rules.

Now they rest on street lamps
before finding

a strip of grass, a small tree
in the shadows of tall buildings
and no people

while you and I are driving,
driving around, following
after them,

you and I boxed in a box
with other boxes,

stuck between lines
where we have to go.

*

The city brightens
before the sky darkens—

the birds, not fooled,
crow in the last sunlight,
land where they land,

and you and I driving,
driving and looking
for a place to park—

something not too far
from a life with wings.

58 Dead In England

The inspectors at Dover found them
slumped behind crates of tomatoes,
Suffocated in the airtight freight-hold
on the hottest weekend of the year.
Five hours across the Channel, the truck's
Refrigeration unit switched off…
The newspapers and TV tell us
they died dreaming a better life.

We all think we know a better life—
we see it shining on the screen—
and sometimes in our own freight-holds,
trapped with the ash-heaps of our longings,
we die dreaming a better life.

Fires Here

Smoke the hunters finally spot
   after frigid days trudging
knee-deep in forest snow:

the warmth of the hearth,
   the heat of a young wife's thighs
over one more heart-shaped hill,

and swirling like smoke
   laughter of curly-haired children
who will hug hard.

But the smoke leads to the pyre
   of villagers slaughtered
by trappers for burning their homes,

the smoke as bilious-black
   as the next burning
of bound heretics,

and then the ash-white smoke
   spewed by incinerators
invented for human flesh,

and all the smoke rising
   away from the earth,
the smoke like incense

escaping a votive candle
   burned to the wick
and beyond it,

the smoke reaching
   a cold black sphere
far from fires here.

Vivisection
Muhamed Fajkovic

'Your black shoes; are you going to wear your black shoes?' my wife Vivian enquires through the slightly open door. If she did come in, she would for a moment have thought she had caught me in the middle of some complicated act of autoeroticism—seeing me lying sideways on the floor in front of the huge dressing mirror that we have in our bedroom, buck naked except for the socks on my feet. But she is too busy even to wait for an answer. Instead she continues down the stairs, shouting: 'They are by the bed'—indicating that the decision was already made on my behalf, and that indeed it's going to be the black shoes. 'I'll have a shower,' her voice fades away, but I can hear the sound of her naked feet slapping against the wooden floor, and then the closing of the bathroom door downstairs. 'Yes,' I shout back, or more precisely, I mimic 'shouting back' because no voice comes out of my mouth. I try once more but my lips don't really move and still no sound comes out, although a bit of saliva does. I try to raise my hand in despair—once again without any success. I try one wretched effort to lift myself up—a silly business really; an effort that as the proclaimed goal has the prospect of me standing up, but in reality only contains the tiniest hope that at least my fingers or my little toe will move ever so slightly. Nothing happens. I'm caught in the clinch by this pain in my chest that's both numb and numbing; but after the ache of novelty has diminished I'm able to study rationally the fact that I'm in the middle of having a heart attack, or brain haemorrhage, or whatever the proper diagnosis is for this pain that holds me lying on the floor immobilised.

I was just about to start dressing for the dinner we were supposed to attend; from the lavish buffet of the garments laid out I managed to pick only a pair of socks when the first stabs pierced my chest and made me sit down on our bed, and then rolled me down on the floor. This invisible force kept ordering me around until my body found the most tolerable position. That I ended lying in front of the mirror might be a good explanation for all this calculating observance and lucid pensiveness that I still posses; the mirror duly reflects and gives me the clear view of my miserable position. It gives me the unique opportunity of being able to watch myself in agony; it allows me to be both observer and participant; a cleric that performs last rites on himself; both the condemned patient and the resigned doctor that watches him; both a lifeless corpse and the scalpel in the quivering hand of the pathologist.

That last comparison makes my mind—that heedless and inaccurate archivist—look for something buried deep in its folders; while rummaging through heaps and debris of all possible things he assures us it's there somewhere (no, we don't throw anything, it's all kept), until he gets lucky and there emerges the scene that happened some 40 odd years ago. There I am, that other me; that younger me that went under my name and had the privilege of having this body when it wasn't yet unblemished by ageing; that faraway I—whom I from this distance judge either too harshly or too leniently—is sited in the dark audience of the local public hall. The audience, us two dozens, is in the dark; weak lights and my moody memory doesn't even illuminate the profile of the girl on my right side— my date. But I recall that between two of us an awkward silence has squeezed in, and we, or I at least, are grateful for the appearance of the compère who looks at us conspiratorially, clears his throat and announces only what we more or less already could read from a small notice by the entrance: 'Tonight, a lecture under the title: "The true Vivisection or Dislayering of a Human Being" will be held by spiritual teacher Conrad Dobrichevsky.' I was equally prepared for a scientific experiment, artistic performance or entertaining magician's act; expecting some kind of bullshitting mumbo-jumbo definitively. The only reason I was there after all was the girl—I can't remember what she was but she certainly wasn't a sceptic, not about anything; not about chirology, horoscopes or slowly-spelling messages of Ouija board; after all the decade and our ages weren't sceptical either.

Why can't I remember the girl's name? Both the romance and the fancy were short-lived, but it still seems insulting (to her? to that former me?) that I can't even remember the name or the face of somebody who occupied my mind so much for a while. Now it's only the silly archivist that vouches for her existence by presenting an unclear shape—a shape that after all might be just a sum of all those female silhouettes from my teenage and youth years; an essence of all those early experiences that an inspired pop lyricist or a helpless self-help books could call "tough lessons in love". But why is it then, when I have forgotten so much, that I remember this lecture; the name and the face of this Conrad Dobrichevsky? Perhaps it's because as soon as he entered stage I could tell that in his appearance there was incorporated a calculated intention to impress: he was wearing an embroidered small hat, a matching robe with girdle around the waistline and big moustaches, as if he deliberately chose to wear the obvious disguise of a charlatan. He looked around with his small eyes, spread his arms, looked at the ceiling for a second and then suddenly announced in thundering voice: 'Caucasus; if the seed of truth is to be found somewhere, it surely must be in the Caucasus; there where religion and people and beliefs mix, clash and coexist as nowhere else.' He looked then around to see what impression his statement made on us; it might have made some impression—although I don't remember what kind; just as I don't remember much of this first part of his lecture. Not even why the Caucasus was so important. I do remember his accent—a strange accent, not completely without its charm. I remember also that he paid homage to his 'master teacher' that he didn't name; any later reference to him sounded as a reference to something more sublime, spiritual and complex than a real blood and flesh human. This master teacher was accredited for originating and handing down to Dobrichevsky something that for the rest of the night was solemnly and ceremonially referred to as the Teachings. Their basic principles I again remember vaguely—no doubt because we were offered only a rather general outlook; and even that probably over the years got mixed with banal philosophising from movie dialogues and those handy wisdoms found in broken fortune cookies. I think though that I can with certainty vouch that this was mentioned: Each individual is seen as a divine form in progress ('we are all but divine seeds in waiting'); necessity of constant challenging of your inner-self ('as if playing chess with yourself'); need for spiritual as well as physical and social development ('all of them equally important'); ecumenical factor ('seed of truth is being sown in each religion, each corner of the world, each myth'). At the end we were offered the very essence of the Teachings: 'which is the constant observance of our own situation; the constant development of all of our beings'.

I observe myself now, smiling bitterly (not literary because I can't order my lips to flatten into a smile), wondering if this is what happens to the divine seed at the end? Does it just fall down, unfulfilled and barren; never achieving its original and intended purpose? Or have I on the contrary made myself superfluous by exactly serving all my purposes to the full? And if that's true why am I then at this moment bothered by these odd and unimportant memories? Is it just a proof of my mind's capricious nature?

'Yes, we have to fight ourselves, to fight our mind's capricious nature,' Teacher Dobrichevsky finished alarmingly after using a good part of lecture on describing and explaining the Teachings—explanations and description that made its principles appear even more vague and incomprehensible. He then made a dramatic pause, looked around as if searching for somebody familiar, somebody who should be recognised, and I sank into my seat, hoping he wasn't looking for volunteers in order to end his lecture with a tremendous magician act. He didn't—instead he lifted his gaze towards the ceiling and declared: 'Ladies and gentleman, I would like to try to illustrate one of the most exciting moment in our teachings—the Concept of True Vivisection or what I call: Dislayering of Human Being.'

The concept that surprises me by its absence right now is the one of retrospective calculus applied on one's whole life. Seeing one's life flying in front of one; all the happy and sad moments, with undeniable positive balance (you were a good father, a good friend, a good…)—all that would give some glamour to the end… But nothing of the sort happens! I comfort myself with the thought that it's possibly because this is not the end—or perhaps it is and this only proves that we end our lives the same way we live them: struggling with the prosaic present, our mind reproducing images from the past or imagining those from the future, all of them being mixed up and muddled…resulting in this humiliating present moment happening parallel, simultaneously with that distant memory. Both are dead serious and side-splittingly comic—nothing illustrates it better then the fact that I'm lying here in agony and at the same time can see how ridiculous these socks on my feet look. Why wasn't I allowed to get dressed completely and then lie on the bed, looking dignified, a glorious example of how to go into that gentle night? Instead, I represent here the bitter irony, the acid comedy, the witty tragedy we live by on the daily basis, and indeed why not the moment like this?

The Teacher continues: 'Dislayering or the real vivisection is the act that should be performed on daily basis. We should cultivate, acknowledge and face the different layers that make and complete ourselves. The old man should be happy for the youngster in himself; the poet should shake hands with the prosaic, penny-pinching bore that he is too; the philosopher should offer a comforting shoulder to himself as a simpleton who sheds tears while listening to sentimental songs about lost love; a stoic should always sit at the table with his twin temperate brother; every layer of us needs attention, needs to be developed. Then, and only then do we make steps forward, leap forward, if you want, towards the true design and designation of our humans.'

No more leaping for this individual, I'm afraid. I'm chained to the floor by the heavy shackles of the physical reality, by this weakness of human flesh—and as if it wasn't more than enough I feel the heavy feeling of guilt is being laid over me. The feeling of guilt that I can't even explain. It is irrational, of course; one of those feelings we can't master and most certainly can't get rid of. I wonder, why guilt? Perhaps Dobrichevsky is right here—underdevelopment of some of our layers gives others an opportunity to expand, and perhaps in dramatic situations like this one the most developed facets prevails—either one that defines us better than any other, or just one that seems most appropriate? I don't know; I have never even learned how to control them or how to generate them intentionally; guilt, maliciousness, pride, generosity or any other human quality were always uninvited guests that would without prior warning knock on the door and insist on sharing my humble home with me.

'Yes, how do we go about it?' Teacher Dobrichevsky asked, 'how do we work on our different layers? We can create ourselves only if we control these different layers that make us; otherwise they will be just uninvited guests or ghosts, if you want, that haunt our homes. But the wish to explain the methods of our Teachings necessarily presents us with the problem of representation—how to illustrate an idea so that's easily grasped?' The seriousness of the Teacher's last words attained somewhat comic connotations, from which the lecture never completely recovered, when at that point two assistants came on the stage carrying a fully dressed tailor's dummy. Laughing murmur came from all sides, but the Teacher didn't seem to be bothered about that—the one that knows the truth is not bothered with displays of petty-mindedness., I suppose. Instead he continued: 'While physicians can use corpses to see the inner workings of a man, the dead man is of no use to us; a dead man contains nothing but just one layer, because the dead body is just an empty shell. Therefore,' he made a gesture to his assistants to bring dummy in front, 'therefore we would have to improvise in order to depict these spiritual layers for you; in order to depict what I chose to call the True Vivisection.' He said all that and smiled for the first time that evening, revealing crooked and yellowish teeth. 'What we have here is a human being as we see it every day,' he ignored the fact that it wasn't exactly a human being we were looking at it, 'its potentials and abilities, of which we are only seldom permitted to catch a rare glimpse, buried deep inside. But,' here he laid his hand on the dummy's shoulder, 'let's not make the easy mistake of believing this outer layer is not important. The outer layer, both clothes and the body, are reflections of everything inside. Not direct reflection, not symmetric dependence, not proportional connection. No; but all I say is that there is a connection.' He then turned suddenly around and addressed his assistants: 'Could we please remove the clothes?'

I look at my own nakedness. Not a pretty sight; a sight whose reflection in the mirror I had avoided for quite some years now. An old man's body. This terrible resemblance to the stranded sea-lion; years adding extra layers of blubbery flesh that I see only too clearly. And that horrible long and grey chest hair that I always founded disgusting. And that enormous belly of mine that I can't even pull in a bit, as I do whenever I'm stricken by a sudden attack of vanity. And my penis, minimized, as if ashamed to have caused so much trouble and frustration in former days; a useless piece of tissue that's now just a mockery of the potent and fertile symbol it used to be. I look into my own eyes—the look is watery and weary.

In the dummy's dead eyes there seemed to be an expression of embarrassment when it suddenly was left standing there naked after the assistant moved a step away from it. It almost assumed the hunchbacked stature of a man that fights desire to cover his intimate parts with his hands—only he is not allowed to do that. An absurd impression, of course, since the dummy didn't even have any genitals. 'Here,' the Teacher moved our attention to the heap of clothes at which he pointed accusingly: 'Here lies the first layer that we hide behind. We acknowledge its necessity, but we see clearly its tendency to become a shield of vanity, the badge of our insecurity.' He paused, before adding: 'But here is the paradox: now that we see a naked man, we are not any closer to his true being. If we could slice through him, layer by layer, we could reveal what a man is made of, but not what he is. Dislayering doesn't mean that there is a core of truth to which we can get closer by removing layer after layer. Very often, it's other way around. Very often we have to put layer after layer on, and then take a closer look by stepping back. We have to put several layers together in order to have a clearer picture and at the same time discard all the layers that distort it.'

I wonder if I've started losing my layers? If they will start falling off now, or if this happened some years ago, and this is the final act, and I will be left with the last one—the empty shell Dobrichevsky mentioned? I hear Vivian coming out of the bathroom—only instead of running upstairs, as I expect, she is fidgeting with something downstairs. First I almost feel annoyance, but then comes pity. Pity that she will find me lying like this; that she will go into the shock. I hope she won't panic, and that she will stay composed enough to call the ambulance right away. I have a dying man here—is that what she is going to tell them?

'In each man different layers can be identified, and that's important to do, if you are to work on them,' Dobrichevsky informed us before proceeding with some of the most bizarre acts I have ever seen. One moment, assistants under Teacher Dobrichevsky's command would put trousers on the dummy; then would strip him naked and put a briefcase into his hand; next, the dummy had a shirt and tie and blazer on, but his legs were left comically nude—and all that in order to illustrate different aspects of a human being. This absurd act, this strange ensemble fidgeting about this dummy, is something I remember as a dream, or as if recollecting scenes from a dramatic silent movie: jerky movements of characters, exaggerated gestures, all being involuntarily funny. The explanations that accompanied these acts, those intertitles that Dobrichevsky provided, those remarks on human nature seen in the light of the Teachings, I don't recall. Sound comes only at the end; the assistants and the dummy are gone and the Teacher stands there alone on the stage, looking dissatisfied with what he just has demonstrated. He is silent for a second or two, but then he reassures us: 'This is just a crude example, a crude sketch of reality. I want you to see beyond that.' He goes silent again, as if he is thinking hard about something and then speaks again: 'Ideally, and I sometimes dream about this, we would find a man that's just about to die—a man not a stranger to our Teaching, perhaps—and then he would perform for us all the different roles he has played, we would see them, obvious ones and then after the death has occurred a team of physicians would perform their kind of vivisection—the bloody one, with scalpels and organs and all that. Perhaps then we would see the complete human being, as it is, perhaps then we would be able to comprehend what a human being consists of in its entirety?'

I'm pleased Teacher is not around, because I do not dare think what he would do with my helpless body here. I'm not sure what would they find anyway. I can't help feeling now, like then, that it all was a load of bollocks. Not because those things were untrue, or because this Dobrichevsky suddenly lost his accent in the middle of the lecture; not because he didn't really give us anything that night, except a bit of entertainment, but because I feel that at the end all the knowledge of the world can't save us from being human. I try to move, but my body still doesn't obey its master. I blink, wondering if I will have to communicate with others in that way, and how long will it take me just to indicate I would like a glass of water. Please! What will become of me in the near future: shall I turn into ash, invalid or spirit? Or shall I rise again, and live?

I don't know if those Teachings survived or if somebody still preaches them somewhere—I never heard of them again. This Dobrichevsky I did see again, some years later, on *Top of the Pops*, playing some kind of tambourine in a rock-band (was it 'Mags of Rock?'). He wore some kind of oriental outfit and had a straight, serious, dedicated and clean-shaved face—no doubt convinced that he was practising one of his layers. Perhaps he was just his own best pupil, following his own plea and the advice he gave us at the very end of his strange lecture that night forty years ago: 'What I want you to take from here tonight is awareness of the possibility to work on yourself. And then use that possibility. Are you ready to do that?'

I hear Vivian's steps. She is coming upstairs! I hear her coming closer and closer. 'Are you ready?' she asks, already by the door, and in the mirror I can see the door opening slowly. For a moment I'm almost afraid Conrad Dobrichevsky with an entourage of assistants, pupils and audience will enter in order to witness the true dislayering of this human being. But I'm relieved as I see the end of Vivian's familiar bathrobe. Then I hear her scream. Then I realise that for some reason I'm still trying hopelessly to crack a smile.

Diana Gittins

Repulsive II

Our first summer at Indian Hill
Dad bought a kit to make a dinghy.
I helped him build it on the lawn, passing
screws and washers as the hull, then seats
took shape. We licked on varnish, painted
the outside with many coats of white.
On the stern in red Mom carefully wrote
Repulsive II, Sakonnet, RI.
It was Dad's idea of a joke.

We launched and moored her at Sakonnet Point.
Dad taught me how to row —
oarlocks, gunwhales, starboard, port and bow —
my arms grew strong and tan.

Dad went away more and more.
I rowed alone.

Towards the end of August the winds blew in.
Branches fractured —
crashed on clapboard. Windows
fissured. Walls
shook. Screaming
spiralled up and down
the chimney. Dishes and pans spun
off shelves — smashed.
The massive elm
uprooted.

After the hurricane left
we piled in the car, drove to the Point
gawped at ripped houses, bathtubs on lawns
anchors and sails strewn across the street,
watermelons bobbing on the calm blue sea.

Hale New Moon Bopp

for Emily

Walking to a Japanese dinner
after speaking too long of madness
(too late to water the garden)
I wondered how long we must wait and
there it was
trailing spindrift over rooftops, chimneys, trees.
I clutched the Chardonnay in awe,
saw three boys pointing to the sky.

I woke to hear my pregnant daughter call
out from my dream like a little girl

thought of my mother
went into the garden
found on its back a camellia
long taken for dead
alive.

I watered it   staked it
now it grows slowly
beside a fat shrub
slowly as we wait
slowly in the wake.

Adrift in grey breeze
monotonous as wood pigeons
the moon sits haloed, a blur of baby's hair

swimming unaware preparing to leap
like a salmon over rocks.

At the edge of the estuary
a whistle of rigging, rock of hull
wide skiff ploughs a murky sea
orange sunset, silver mud

body and skin strong and whole.

Judith Watts

Smiling Torso/Laughing Buttocks

Bronze, Dora Gordine, 1937-8, Dorich House Museum

My child? No. Not this one.
This one was born into awakening.
Her skin mottled and moist, shines with the patina of sweat.
See where I stretched her pelvis with the heels of my hands?
Where I opened her thighs with my thumbs
Where my fingers formed cracks and dimples.
Stroke the haunch, her hip bone pushes like a crocus through earth.
I know what's inside; how to hollow, to possess,
fill with molten wax until air flows instead of veins
inside the empty frame. I hold her together
mould, chased seams, press indentations,
coax her imperfect body from its shell
leaving the head in slurry.

Will Kemp

Wolf

The wolf's howl consists of a single note
which may contain as many as twelve related harmonics;
it rises in sharp crescendo and then breaks off abruptly.

You can hear it now, long and low,
      alone,

as the moon clears

and the great unknown spreads out
      in silvered folds,

the frozen lake a star-sprinkled glow,

stalagmite trees pointing north
      like Eskimo whalebone spears,

where the shadows seem to move
      with something faint—

but there,
      through the soft and powdered snow—

a percussion of panting
          with padded feet.

Orpheus

after Paterson after Rilke after Ovid

In the forest, a clearing
steeped in light.
And at its centre, seated,
a man, head bowed.
All was still.
And then he touched the lyre.

One by one they came,
from every fox-hole, nest and lair,
not drawn by scent,
or out of fear or stealth,
but the sound
of slow notes pouring through the air.

Without a growl or snarl,
they sat about the ground—
lion, vixen, deer—
each looking down
with eyes that knew his loss,
and understood now what it was to feel.

The painters who studied clouds

From my window I am watching the sky drift by
in white and grey across the blue,
with dabs of lemon-yellow here and there,
where the sun glows a while
but never quite comes into view.

It makes me think of the painters who studied clouds,
no camera to catch the changing scene,
sitting alone in a field, or tied
to a mast in the howling storm,
rolling sea and sky into one great swirl.

How quickly they must have worked
in silverpoint or chalk,
sometimes snowblind from taking in the light,
hatching rounded shapes with shade
to give the sky its full-blown form and tone,

at others cursing it for cirrus clouds,
moving as slow as ocean whales,
to let a sweep of wash
beach on the wet paper, or seep
into a distant summer haze.

I wonder then if they too wondered
at Constable's *Painting of Clouds*,
with its bulk of greys and half-greys,
windswept with hurried brushes,
sailing across and out the frame,

seeing how he must have looked and looked,
until he understood
the light, tone and shapes as one—
then took them down at once,
knowing in a moment they'd be gone.

Offerings and Thanksgivings
Janet Swinney

Ramesh sat on the cot on the roof, one leg swinging idly to and fro. The sun was still bright, but had slipped into a cooler part of the sky. Ramesh breathed deeply. He had had a hard day at the bazaar, selling shoes to choosy customers, making sure their every wish was met. This was the time of day he appreciated: time to reflect on the day's efforts, time to contemplate the way of the world. His leg kept up its meaningless, comforting motion. The cot creaked beneath him.

The door to the roof opened. It was his wife, Nirmala, bringing him a glass of tea. With her came the waft of household smells: phenol and soap. She walked towards him with the hot glass. He looked up and stretched out his hand to take it. She kept her eyes from him, not deliberately, but as though she had nothing positive to offer, as though all dialogue went on within her, behind that tired, sagging face. The moment before he should have grasped the glass, she let it slip through her fingers and so, through his. It shattered on the ground, spraying his foot with scalding tea and splinters. He gasped in surprise. Nirmala surveyed the deed, then turned and wordlessly walked back the way that she had come. She stepped into the house. The door closed behind her.

Ramesh sighed. He wiped the tea from his foot with the bottom of his pyjama. Without clearing up the mess, he swung both his feet up on the cot and sat thinking. His wife hadn't always been like this.

They had been happily married at first. It had been an arranged marriage. The first years had been spent making the adaptations and adjustments that are a necessary part of learning to live with another person. It had been an uncomfortable, but intriguing adventure through which both their families had supported them. After two or three years, people had begun to ask, 'Where are the children?' Nirmala took no notice at first. She was still a pretty girl, interested in making the most of herself and in finding out about her own personality. These things, the pretence that at some point she might become a 'working lady' and occasional, painful disagreements with her husband kept her fully occupied.

Then she had her twenty-sixth birthday. Friends of her own age and younger had had their first child and were busy with their second or third. Nirmala scrutinised these small ones closely. She watched them lying on their backs, smiling unfocusedly and abstractedly waving their arms. She observed them struggling to their feet to take their first staggering steps. She became fascinated by the fact that life arises, that it arises unasked for and that each arising is its own pattern-in-the-making. The nudges of her sisters-in-law started to annoy her. The constant enquiries of visitors to the house sent her into the bedroom to cry in rage. The having of a child became a serious business.

Nirmala's parents were simple and straightforward. Much of their outlook on life had been inherited from those who had gone before them. They lived within their means and unthinkingly put their faith in the gods, hard work and sayings like: 'You can scrub a donkey with soap, but it'll never be a cow', 'Only action is in one's hands, and not its fruit' and 'You can't live in the river and upset the crocodiles'. In times of trouble such things were a constant source of comfort and guidance. Nirmala's mother fasted every Tuesday, never touched onions or garlic and always kept a portion of food aside for the birds. Every day, she visited the temple to leave flowers or some other sort of offering. Nirmala had naturally adopted some of these habits. Now, when times were bad, Ramesh noticed her spending more and more time at the temple. He had seen her once through the gate, muttering to herself and pacing round and round the idol, totally preoccupied. She said that she had made a pact with her god: that if he would allow her to conceive, the remainder of her life would be spent in his service. Ramesh wasn't certain how to receive this and, not being certain, said nothing.

In the meantime, they visited the doctors—many doctors, and many clinics. There was nothing wrong with Ramesh, it seemed. The problem lay somewhere with Nirmala. Finally the homoeopath, who had less than usual to do that day, lay back in his chair, picked his teeth and said it was a difficult case: he had seen it all before—Nirmala was a typical sepia patient—but that this sort of thing was a speciality of his, and if they'd leave it all to him, he'd see what he could do. They were only too glad to leave it all to someone. Nirmala came away from the surgery loaded down with prescriptions, pillules and bottles.

The months passed. Nirmala kept up her daily rituals and her medication. She had started saying that if she were granted a child she would make a pilgrimage of thanks to the holy Ganga. Ramesh listened to this nervously, knowing that money was scarce.

Then, when she was twenty-nine, she conceived. She came back from the homoeopath's with the pregnancy confirmed, fell into her mother-in-law's arms and cried with joy. Indeed, her mother-in-law shed tears of joy too. Soon, the talk was of nothing but the trip to the River Ganga. Ramesh, feeling the weight of his newly-acquired responsibility, tried to dissuade them: the journey to Hardwar would be too much for his wife, the child ought to be given every chance to develop in peace and comfort, the cost of the venture would be far too much for them now that they had the future of their unborn child to think about. However, Nirmala would not entertain these views. She had made her promise to her god and now her wish had been granted, she was duty-bound to offer thanks. Her mother-in-law, who sympathised with this line of thinking, supported her throughout their arguments. Nirmala worked herself into such a frenzy every time that Ramesh tried to broach the subject, that in the end he felt it would be safer for all concerned if he gave his consent. It was agreed that his mother would accompany them on their excursion to keep an eye on Nirmala's well-being.

They set out at nine o'clock one spring morning. The air was fresh with anticipation. Ramesh wore a shirt that was stiff with pressing. The women's saris rippled in the cool morning breeze. They hired a couple of rickshaws from outside the house, and Ramesh's younger sister waved them out of sight.

The bus station, as always, was very busy. There was the usual pushing and shoving, the usual buying and selling, the usual squalor and finery. There were travellers travelling a couple of miles up the road to the next village, and travellers like themselves setting out upon some major expedition.

They bought their tickets, had their luggage loaded on top of the bus, then struggled on board to find some seats. They were lucky: they found three together. Gradually, the remaining seats filled with passengers. They, meantime, filled their laps with chole and oranges in readiness for their journey. Finally, at ten o'clock, amid uncalled for fuss and strident hooting, the bus thrust its way out on to the road.

The passengers soon became used to the pattern of the journey: long stretches of highway laid like a strap across the countryside where people and cattle turned their unending circles in the fields; unremarkable towns where, at the roadside, men made their slow and effortful attempts at industry. Out on the highway, the driver bared his teeth, put his foot to the floor and sent scooters and cycles wavering into the undergrowth. Sometimes, on a power-crazed whim, he overtook some obstacle and brought them face-to-face with an oncoming vehicle of overwhelming proportions. At the last minute, he would stand on the brake to avoid an accident. The passengers would be flung into new positions where, as their alarm subsided, they settled to await the next crisis. Their progress through the towns was even more erratic. They trod at the heels of ambling pedestrians, threatening their lives. They roared through bazaars, intervening in business transactions. They became needlessly involved with bullock carts and all other forms of transport. And all the while, the driver wrung shrill agony from the horn. Every fifth town or so they would pull into a bus station, and there would be a changeover of passengers. Otherwise, they stopped on bridges and at roundabouts and anywhere else which would create confusion.

There was great discomfort for Nirmala. The seats were close together and it was difficult for her to change position. They had not gone many miles from home when every window in the bus rattled shut. As the sun crawled into its inevitable position in the sky, the air became stale and lifeless. The smell began to nauseate her. At every stop the conductor took on more passengers than he could cope with. They clung to whatever they could find, with their elbows in each other's sides and their feet in awkward positions. The woman behind Nirmala fell asleep and her head fell heavily on Nirmala's back. But Nirmala bore all of this because of the goal that she pursued. She constantly reminded herself of the child she was carrying and of the gratitude she owed. In this way, she managed to keep a grip on level-headedness.

Acacia trees became palm trees and palm trees acacia. Women piled dung cakes by the walls of their dwellings. Vultures held convocation in the tops of barren trees. In the fields, the people worked chopping down sugar cane and piling it on to carts. On the outskirts of towns, surrounded by the debris of mangled cane, were the mills where the carts stood empty. Their chimneys gave off an idle smoke that refused to drift heavenwards. The sullen eyes of the open furnaces glowed along their walls. The sweet, repellent smell of molten sugar penetrated even the bus and rendered the air palpable. Eventually the sun sank among the furnaces. A few, trailing clouds caught the last reflection and then it was night.

They were set down in a village outside the town. Ramesh's mother had a cousin there who hadn't seen her for years. People moved about in the light shed by the lamps at tea-stalls and on peanut vendors' barrows. The scene was no different from that in their own home town. Yet, through the darkness, they sensed the strangeness of this new, far place. Ramesh's mother's cousin welcomed them with open arms. She gave them a meal and left them to sort out their bedding.

They awoke next morning much refreshed. Now that they were here with so much of their mission accomplished, they were in no hurry to bring it to a close. They lay savouring the sounds around them. Even the clank of the pump in the yard seemed new and endowed with special qualities. Outside in the street people exchanged the day's gossip in an accent that was, amazingly, not their own. Even Ramesh was caught up in the excitement of the place and felt his spirits stirring.

They set out late in the morning when the sun was already pinned high in the sky. They took a bus into town then, following their relative's brief instructions, began the walk to the ghat through streets that were thronged with people. The everyday activity of small town life was augmented by the comings and goings of numerous pilgrims. Tongas bowled past them bearing whole families swathed in their best nylons and chiffons. There were sadhus with the look of many weeks' travelling about them, touting their bundles; the lame and the blind, their faces set determinedly, hobbling along towards salvation and, here and there among the crowd, the grey face of an undernourished Western traveller. The shops sold things they were not familiar with. Nirmala stopped to some garlands and some coconut for the shrines. She hung the garlands over her arm.

The air seemed iridescent, imparting an extra dimension, a

clarity and a depth of colour they had never seen before. What, in their own town, would have seemed a bother and a nuisance here seemed cheerful and pleasing. They became infected by the gaiety of the place, talked without listening, laughed without reason. It was as though they were intoxicated. In this frame of mind they continued until the street made a sudden turn and there, before them, was the valley of the Ganga. They stopped in their tracks. The floor of the valley was a broad expanse of sand crossed and counter-crossed by suspension bridges and pontoons. On the far side were hills ranked with tidy greenery. By their feet whipped the channel of cold, green glacier water which was all there was of the sacred river at this time of year. Distances seemed infinite and negligible by turn. Sometimes it seemed possible to reach out and touch the trees on the opposite hills, or to step down and walk across one of the longest bridges, but a glance at the misty horizon with its hint of an untold beyond gave a measure of another sort.

Below them on the steps of the ghat people were lowering themselves into the water. All self-consciousness was forgotten in the pleasure of fulfilling a shared ambition. The young bathed next to the old, the almost-naked next to the fully-clad. The men's bodies sparkled in the sunlight, laced with water; the women's were shrouded in their clinging, flimsy clothing. Their laughter and shouting was snatched from their mouths and lost under the wide, limitless sky. The three of them stood for a long time, their eyes swivelling to and fro—from foreground to middle distance, from middle distance to horizon—completely absorbed in the scene. At last they looked at each other and nodded in agreement: it was their turn to go down to the water.

They began the climb down from the road slowly enough, but their excitement grew and their pace quickened. Nirmala was soon at the bottom. Ramesh came more slowly, steadying his mother. Nirmala paused to get her bearings, then frisked off over the stone bridge to the ghat. Ramesh, with his mother puffing and panting, brought up the rear. Nirmala chose a place on the ghat near two girls in bright saris who were holding their noses and totally submerging themselves in the water. Quickly, she stepped out of her chappals and then, turning to Ramesh, smiled a broad smile of pleasure. With his free hand he struggled to make a movement that meant, 'Yes, I see you. But wait, wait for me,' but she turned back and without more ado, stepped on to the glassy steps that went down into the water.

Quicker than thinking, she had lost her footing. She heard her head hit the stone as though it were somebody else's problem. Then the icy fingers of the water grasped her poor, jolted body and swiftly pulled her under. The two girls reached out in frail gestures of surprise. By the time they hauled her from the water, her sari was already stained with blood.

That night, as on every other night, pilgrims gathered on the steps of the ghat. In a great, metaphoric celebration of the transitory nature of life, they placed fragile boats of leaves and flowers on the black waters of the river and watched, until the lighted tapers within faltered and went out or were swept away into the dwindling distance.

Nirmala, in the meantime, lay in a room at Ramesh's mother's cousin's house tended by the two women and the doctor, a thin, nervous man who did not inspire confidence. Ramesh stalked about the other rooms smoking impatiently. The baby was lost, that he knew, but he was more worried about Nirmala herself.

They made the journey back to their home town two weeks later. This time it was a very different matter. Nirmala had spent most of the two weeks in prolonged bouts of grieving. Now she looked tired and miserable. She sat with her face turned towards the window, her gaze never travelling beyond the stained yellow glass.

At home, they began the long haul back towards normality. Yet somehow, normality was never reached and perhaps it was foolish to think it ever could be. Nirmala's fits of weeping became less frequent and relatives maintained a diplomatic silence on the subjects of child-bearing and rearing. Gradually her manner brightened and everyone took hope. But—it became apparent—the change was only superficial. Her gaiety was brittle and unnerving, a contrived expression of absolute rigidity. She went about her housework with a conscientious fury unequalled by the other women and, several times a day now, left what she was doing and went off to the temple. If anything interfered with her daily schedule her anger was uncontrollable. Once, when an old friend of Ramesh's father's turned up unexpectedly after a day's travelling from the hills, she left the menfolk without any food and disappeared from the house.

She explained quietly to Ramesh one night as he sat on the edge of the bed that if she had not been able to bear their child it was because, for some reason, she had been judged unworthy. Her task was now to double her efforts and prove her worthiness so that the gods would favour her.

It took Ramesh some time to realise what his wife was doing. Once it had occurred to him that she had constructed this narrow system of values as a means of coping with her tragedy he was aghast. He tried to intervene in her obsessive activity to tell her that she was wrong and to say that there must be some other way of dealing with this sorrow. But it was no good. She refused his attention. Her energetic pursuit of worthiness intensified. She made larger and larger offerings at the temple and made gifts to any beggar who passed the door. She gave away food, money, clothes—her own and everyone else's—delicacies he brought home for the family table, trinkets his family had accumulated over the years, a picture his sister had embroidered for the wall, the first crop of fruit from their guava tree. One night he came home and found she'd given away his graduation suit. Every member of the family vented their wrath on her, but she was impervious to it. Over the years he watched her lay bare their household, he felt that the fruit of his efforts at the shoe shop were spent in the upkeep of every unfortunate in the neighbourhood.

Ramesh sat on the outside of his wife's grief and looked helplessly in. In the night she cried out. She mourned for the love she could have given, for the only passion she had known—and lost. In her dreams her breasts grew heavy with longing, her belly swelled in hope of the presence that would take hold at the root of her being. Ramesh shed his own silent, rolling tears. He knew he could not receive this great gift of her love, nor did he have a gift of his own to make. Their relationship was based on necessity and respect. He reproached himself, even as his wife silently reproached him, for not having the need to abandon himself to such desperate emotion. They continued the ritual of husband and wife. In bed Nirmala was vigorous, demanding and entirely self-centred. She completely used him up. Friends of the family commented on her vivacious good humour and listened, bewildered, to her bright-eyed chatter about duty and its rewards. Only Ramesh knew of the anguish that wracked her dreams.

Eventually, as time passed and there was no sign of another child, people looked at her pityingly and said what a shame it was. Nirmala held on till the very last, hoping against hope. When the time came and there was no chance left, he waited with bated breath to see what would erupt. There was nothing. Months passed. Nirmala was mute. Then very suddenly she stopped her visits to the temple, and stopped handing out half their daily diet to beggars in the street. She took her medicine bottles out into the yard and smashed them into a bucket. She came home one day with her face and hands mysteriously covered with bruises. She had obviously decided that the gods had played her false, but she said not a word. She drudged round the house as a matter of course. Her hair straggled loose and her saris were unkempt. Her silence was as discomfiting as her talkativeness had been.

Ramesh sat pondering on the cot on the roof. There were now only the two of them in this crumbling house of his forefathers. Nirmala was forty-eight and there had been no change. The sky grew dark. There was a sudden, chill gust of wind and the parrots rushed from the neighbouring tree-tops to perform their evening circuits. Ramesh got up to fetch a broom. Inside Nirmala a tremendous anger raged. He waited with trepidation for the day when it would break.

Sharon Black

Domestic

She tidies as if at prayer,
pulls soft years from her pockets
and rubs them
into warm floorboards.

The head of a doll
rolls from behind a chair.
She lifts it in her duster
and holds it to the light.

Its eyes are colourless,
paint is flaked from its face;
its neck is a blunt instrument
in her hand.

Sunlight clips her cheek bones
rucking shadows across her brow.
She pulls herself up,
smarts against the glare

and, for a moment, catches sight
of a child, running.

Morning After

She arches back as far as she can reach;
her throat is a pale bridge
stretching from her chest to the moon.

Her fingers ache from touching him;
the veins on the back of her hand protrude
like twine, unravelled, almost frayed.

She traces his outline, tastes his salt,
her tongue tightening.
Among the creases she finds a hair;

held to the square light of day
it bends from her like bulrush,
caught in a squall.

She draws the sheets around her like tissue,
balls them close as if to protect
something fragile, something about to

slip from its wrapper.

Sea Glass

He spends his days sifting pebbles,
rough hands separating
bladderwrack from driftwood,

and holds each piece the light,
runs his thumb around its edges:
buffed, smooth, exotic as polished nails.

He collects them all—moss-green, ice-blue,
opaque as milk, luminous as fish—
drops them in his pocket, counts each chink.

They settle in the darkness like eyes,
nudge his groin
through the coarse cotton lining.

Their shift and chime
echo his step, the sough of the sea
as he crosses the shore.

Later he sets them in rows
like mermaid scales
or a colour chart for frost.

Deborah Harvey

Wronged

I shall not be killing our children,
or sending your mistress a dress
embroidered with poison.
I'd sooner knit nettles into coats
and with stung fingers pluck love
from under a smother of feathers.

I shall not seek deathlessness through death,
or revenge in a vaporous breath that draws me
under winter's ice and snow.
I shall not be penning flayed poems
or prose: it seems that
the market's been cornered in those.

I shall not be mislaying my mind
or drowning in melancholy songs
of love betrayed and squalid wrongs.
There's rue for you, but none for me.
I'm through with flowers and memories.
I'll weave my freedom in my hair.

A Falling of Feathers

for Elizabeth

This morning a falling of feathers:
death as a blessing on soundless wings

I remembered
red feathers on crazy paving,
a ring dove,
the leonine gleam
of a sparrowhawk's fixed eye.
A meeting with fate on an urban savannah.
Two weeks later you nearly died.

This morning I found you
in the kitchen. This time you'd awakened,
partaken of manna
to balance your blood.
While you rested, I hefted
this handful of feathers
against the other, filled with life,

the feathers as soft and grey
as undefined horizons.

The Visitors
Tricia Durdey

I'm in the yard closing the chicken coop for the night. The sun is setting below the hill and the light strikes the hawthorn tree with brilliance, so for a moment its berries stand out like beads of blood and I'm entranced by the intensity of colour. It's then that I sense I'm being watched and I look up and see them standing by the gate, a woman with a child clinging to her arm. I'm not expecting visitors. People never come without invitation. The four o'clock bus has gone from the village and there's nothing but wilderness beyond this house. I can smell the coming of snow.

I should send them away but I can't. Where will they go? The woman doesn't ask for anything, but the child's eyes beg me. I let them in.

I make tea for them. The woman sits upright and self-contained at the kitchen table.

'My name is Frieda, and this is Grace,' she says. The little girl is wearing a green velvet party dress, too big for her, old fashioned with a lace collar. She has a frayed satin ribbon in her hair.

'We won't trouble you for long. Grace's father will come for us.'

Frieda doesn't say more and I'm not inclined to ask.

I do everything I can for them. I make up the beds in the attic and fill hot water bottles. I warm leek soup and serve it in the best china with bread and cheese. I run the bath and leave fresh towels. I'm tired when I go to bed but I lie awake for a long time. The house feels unsettled. My hands and feet are ice cold.

'Charlotte, it's your home,' I tell myself the next morning. 'Today the father will come for them.' But the day wears on and nobody comes. I find myself gazing through the window, anxiety gnawing at my stomach.

'Please use the phone if you need to contact him,' I say to Frieda.

Frieda shakes her head.

'I can't do that. He will come. We have to learn to be patient.'

'Does he know where you are?'

She stares at me. I have to look away. My voice rings in the silence.

Two more days pass. Snow falls and I sweep it away from the door and throw salt and grit along the path. The chickens huddle together, the wind bites. I can't send my strange visitors out in this. The little girl plays alone. She draws pictures on the scrap paper I give her and passes them to her mother. Her mother takes them silently. It's always the same picture in heavy black crayon, of trees and the moon and a lonely figure.

I telephone a friend. I need to speak to someone, but her line is dead. The snow has cut me off. I try to phone an engineer but the numbers jump around and my fingers tremble too much to dial. I pace around the kitchen. I bake bread, pounding at the dough to keep my hands busy.

What is expected of me? Nobody comes for them. I don't know how to make them go. I see my Grandmother, her rigid back, the black leather bible. I must try to be good, tolerant, understanding. Isn't that what you tried to teach me, Grandmother, with your impeccable life and your God?

A day later they need clean clothes. I lend Frieda one of my Grandmother's starched blouses, a grey skirt. I discover a box of clothes I had as a child for Grace and she pounces on it with delight, tossing the clothes out onto the floor. Their underwear soaks in a bucket, then hangs to dry by the fire.

'Frieda, you've been here a week, is there any possibility…' my voice catches in my throat. She looks at me. Her face is lined with such grief that words stop. I see with horror that she's weeping silently, her mouth tight with pain.

'Tell me what it is?' I ask sharply. Stop the tears for pity's sake.

She shakes her head and turns away.

'Shall I put the radio on?'

I switch it on, twiddling the knob between channels, searching for anything to distract me from her pain. Voices. Music. Viennese Waltzes. Grace flings out her arms and laughs. She slides off the chair where she's been sitting with her box of crayons so suddenly that the crayons spill over the floor. She twirls around the room. Her skirt spins outwards.

'Mummy likes me to dance, don't you,' she says in a high voice, 'like this and this.' She lifts her arms over her head and extends a bony leg. She looks grotesque. I grip the mantelpiece. Outside the snow whirls round and round as if it might drift through the glass and into the room choking us.

If it were spring I would open the window. I would pick the bluebells and bring them in, bleeding their sticky sap, their sweet scent. The rapeseed would stain the fields a startling yellow.

I hear my Grandmother's voice. I must have compassion. I write compassion in blue ink a hundred times until I forget what it means and only hear the sound of it beating in my ears. Compassion compassion compassion. An explosion in my head shocks me. A migraine coming. I try to light the fire. We're very cold. But tonight the kindling is damp and it won't take. I go to bed early. It will be different in the morning.

I dream music and wake to hear the piano. Downstairs Grace is picking out notes, singing a skipping song in a high thin voice.

Salt, pepper, vinegar, mustard,
French almond rock,
Bread and butter for your supper,
That's all mother's got…

It has gone midnight. She should be in bed. I pull the quilt over my head. Somehow I sleep again and am woken abruptly to someone pulling at me. I call out and jump up. The lamp is already on. Grace is standing shivering in the pink pyjamas I used to wear when I was six.

'Come quickly. Mummy is ill.'

Frieda lies on top of the bed. Her face, her hands, her whole body where I can see it has erupted in red sores. Where she's scratched they ooze yellow pus and blood. She will not let me touch her.

'You need a doctor.'

She turns her face to the wall.

The room has a strange sweet smell. It makes me nauseous. I stand helpless my hands by my side.

'Go away,' she mutters.

We creep out of the room. Grace clings to my arm.

The house is filled with sadness. The drifts of snow hold us in so nobody can escape. Grace crawls into bed with me. The bedclothes weigh us down.

'Don't cry, please.'

Where does the sadness come from? Grace twists and turns around the bed. It's hard to breathe. 'Please please don't cry I can't bear it, I can't bear it...' She clings to me and I lie rigid.

Dawn comes, a sickly yellow light reflected in the mirror. There's a shout from upstairs, a look of terror on Grace's face. I run up to Frieda. She's pacing around the room.

'Let me out, let me out.' She stands at the open window, her breath ragged, desperate. I grab hold of her wrists and pull her back to bed, but she fights me away. We wrestle, her face up close, her tangled hair, those eyes, the wounded mouth. It's a long time. I don't think I can hold her longer.

Then it's over. All tension falls away and she crumples onto the floor. I lead her back to bed, wrap her in the sheets, and hold her wretched body.

'I can't go on,' she says, sobbing.

I know.

I crawl from the room and slump on the stairs. Grace is standing on the landing. She's found a moth-eaten fox fur and hung it around her neck.

'Mummy doesn't like me. She's very sad.' She gazes up at me.

'I'm sure she loves you, only she's ill. It's very hard to look after someone when you're so ill,' I whisper.

'Will you be my Mummy?'

No.

I push past her down the stairs, pace from room to room. Everything smells of their sickly skin. My head is filled with the buzzing of wasps. No breathing space. How to love, how to love? Granny with your bitter eyes, don't quote God at me. Nothing, nobody to hold onto to stop falling into the void, and God watches and laughs. I walk out of the door. It's over.

Blood and feathers lie in the snow. I didn't shut the chickens away last night and the fox has taken them all. My poor beauties! How could I forget?

I walk for a long time in darkness. It is so lonely. In the silence I hear them breathing, Frieda and Grace, but I keep on walking. I walk until it's over. My feet ache to the bone.

It's late spring when I can go home at last. The lane is drowned in May blossom and lilac, the heavy blooms, the scent I want to draw into me. Oh it is over and I am glad! I go from room to room, opening all the windows and singing. In the morning I strip the beds and wash the sheets. They billow on the line between the apple trees under a blue sky.

Today I plant saplings in the orchard, cherry, pear, and almond. There is a quiet calm, full of anticipation of something too lovely, too exquisitely beautiful to imagine. Something is waiting. I crouch down to pull the weeds from around the old trees. Everywhere is alive with colour and sound. I have gone through the eye of a needle. Grandmother, you would never understand. We are different, you and I.

I hear a voice and turn to look.

'Will you be my Mummy?'

I press my hands into the earth and listen intently. There is nobody there.

Gillian Craig

Odd Comfort

In Taoyuan
We watched them go by.
A coffin truck, neon and desolate.
Another with a band clattering
A dirge in its fullest sense.
Jarring, or at least
Unsyncopated.

In Hanoi
We watched them go by.
A coffin bus with an open back door,
Flanked by white-scarved mourners.
Instruments shrieking and skirling.
Tuneless, or at least
Indefinable.

In Bangkok
They watched us go by.
A last whisper as we placed
A candle and a flower with the coffin.
Monks intoned, our conduits.
Wordless, or at least
Incomprehensible.

And this, at least, makes sense.
Because the rhythm has been lost.
Because there is no tune we could sing.
Because there are no words for this.

Annie Bien

Beneath night

between the stars,
I place my head,
listen to space:

your hand combs
your hair, points
to the pillar
seemingly so solid:
steers us to an image
of a smiling golden buddha
who reveals light
through fanned fingers.

Imagine
what goes beyond
the words, the labels
side by side,
the fullness
between the lines:
where the shape
of my face
falls into the hollow,
where your eye
absorbs mine.

Clear skies, swift clouds

謝 *In Chinese: to wilt, to thank, to decline.*

I remember the first day I remembered:
On the left—black—on the right—a square of light.
My mother's foot pushes a doll away,
leather shoe against my pudgy leg.
I turn to the dark side, nothing
draws me back. I put my head
into the bright box. My mother's face
searches elsewhere, distracted
from the child on her lap, her gaze
fixed on an imaginary horizon,
an escape from the present.

I didn't know her eyes wept
for liana twined banyan trees,
the tissue under her armpits dampened
her search for intoxication by gardenia.
She unhooks the collar of her cheongsam,
closes her eyes, flies to the land where blossoms
never wilt, and jasmine wafts under eyelids:

Flowers wilt, *xie*: 謝.
You say thank you:
xie xie, 謝謝
Repeated twice, it brings double
grief. Because when you thank someone,
you apologize. You wilt twice and bow.
She could never see the azalea bloom
without seeing the petals scattered on the ground.

No footstep left, she leaves
an embrace, a parting, wilting.
Her diaries contain small cursive
notes for lost days. In the sunlight,
bees swarm in gratitude to a camellia—
petals speckled in a dance of pollen.

Help in Case of Accidents:

6. Tests of Death:

*with extracts from Carboloy Cemented Carbides datebook 1949, my mother's
journal*

Hold mirror to mouth. If living, moisture will gather.

Your neck vibration subsides.
The nurse doesn't hold a mirror.

Push pin into flesh

I don't own any pins.
The nurse presses a stethoscope
against translucent skin.

*If dead the hole will remain,
if alive it will close up.*

The nurse holds your jaw
shut with a gloved hand —
your mouth falls open again.

Your jaw, once so tense
formed a puckered chin
and sealed lips.

Now you let the secrets
escape through inkstained notebooks,
sighs fall from the pages.

Heart 心

心 *In Chinese: heart, mind*

Nightflower petals
unfurl to moon

I hide your smile
in my pulse:

more than blood
runs through my veins,
the current of your breath
mingles honey
melted in heat.

Three tear drops suspend
over a cradle:
when we first met
when we meet
when we meet again.

Traveller's tales

A traveller without observation is a bird without wings
—*quotation, 1954, 1955 date book*

Focus on mom the traveller!
—*Robert Thurman*

In the west,
where the sun sets
beyond the horizon
above our universe
beyond our moon, sun, stars,
beyond our universe—our one unit
of universe—this you know by now
since you can travel unhindered,
having shed your body—you zoom up,
down, on diagonal—north, south, east,
travel west, toward the sunset—
multiply our universe by one thousand
times one thousand times one
thousand times.

That's how you need to consider travel,
not so far because distance is relative:
you were once an accountant,
so all that multiplying is a cinch,
and when you arrive so far west,
you'll step into *Sukhavati,* Land of Ultimate Bliss.

Here it rains flowers six times a day:
trees are made of gold, silver, beryl,
crystal, coral, red pearl, and diamonds.
Remember those birds that I mentioned
last night, they are a manifestation of messages
from *Amitabha,* the Buddha of Infinite Light,
your guide through their avian songs.
People there smile the way you did
to me when we said hello
that last time when we spoke
your fingers gripped and your heart burst

into a lotus, though the petals fell away.

I fill my skull with bright light
pour rays through my heart and out
my toes. Tomorrow I'll tell you more.

The New Café
Margaret Wilmot

It's been so long. Your letters are in a jumble, and I can't find a last date. Hoping you're still there, I'm writing to the new café, which was such a shock on my last visit fifteen years ago. Huge and glistening, it assumed its place like some tragic heroine before the useless crowd to state: I have made my choice; what takes place now is mine.

I'm writing to a woman in black behind a marble counter, reaching for coffee, perhaps, and putting on a briki, or weighing out rice, potatoes, locating vanilla, pencils, razor-blades on the crowded shelves behind you. If people still use the café as a shop. Maybe they have cars, drive off to Erimantheia, even Patras—the new road cut off so many bends. Or have died. Are you still in mourning? First your father, then your brother... You wrote of going to Germany to see Labis in hospital—and I wondered, did the café shut? Who else can do your job? Your father remains vivid in my mind, thin and funny as he was when I first came, and we all ate and laughed together with your mother and the schoolmaster too; it was your father started our little ritual each night as I pushed back my chair to go:

'Good night,' I'd say.

'Sleep well,' he'd respond, nodding his head sideways, and grinning to hold me there.

'Sweet dreams,' I quickly learned to add.

'Sweet dawn,' he would conclude, triumphantly, and again we'd all be laughing.

Much later came the image of him shaving under the café vine, mirror propped against his cup of foam—he scraped unsteadily, somehow childlike in the morning light. Then one warm night his silver hair caught the full moon as he wandered down the road instead of over to the house. You came out of the café, and stared, and unnerved ran crying after him, 'Father! Father!' He took to offering round the cigar-box where you dropped people's drachmas, 'Have some!' he'd nod genially, still playing host. Yet his death left you desolate. I didn't understand then how when someone you love dies you miss not the last hard times but the whole shimmering life which is still part of yours.

There was so much I didn't understand, Maroula. Your letters seemed like poems which opened windows on a pain Aeschylus might have given voice: Cassandra's pain, aware both of the horrific moment, and all that lay ahead. You even signed them 'I kiss you with love and pain.' The words were real as stones, and I couldn't grasp their weight. Coming as I did from somewhere there was always choice, even too much—like your father passing round the box of drachmas—it took me years to accept the absoluteness of necessity, how lives are shaped by birth, geography, the times, and that the ways you had to fight were very limited. And who said, 'Character is destiny?' None of the other village women took the care you did, picking the tiniest specks out of the cauldron simmering with May milk for the year's cheese; embroidering so both sides of the pattern were equally fine; whitewashing—your house got two coats, and the porch had oil tins of geraniums and basil. Once I brought you bulbs and you were thrilled, and later on flowers painted by my sister-in-law; you had the picture framed and hung it between the purple sunset and the Virgin encrusted with small shells.

You draw water, and thistles become green around the well.
You call, and children come running from their games.
You sew gold sequins on your scarf; the sky trembles with stars.
You sigh, and a wave surges down through the olives.

What made your life tragic was precisely this fineness of perception, whatever the work, whatever the consequences; one made that choice, for the greater wholeness of things, despite all cost. 'What about the cafe? Who would help my parents?' you asked wearily when someone wanted you to work in Athens, and I was saying 'Go, Maroula—it won't be as hard as here!' Your siblings had escaped; sometimes they sent money—you bought a fridge for the café the moment the village got *the current*, offered cold drinks. You bought yourself an electric iron. But the money, though useful, was hardly the main thing. I visited and played the clown, thinking she needs to laugh—but that was hardly the main thing either.

As usual, you put a briki on for me when I last came. I sat in the huge and airy place which changed everything around it, including my perception of the unmarried self who used to come so long before. She seemed unconscious, naïve, insubstantial as the shadows in the old café, (shrunk to a storeroom now): gone too the card-players, the politics, the stove brought in for winter, and the schoolmaster holding his newspaper in the circle of white light beneath the lamp to read aloud—all those shouts and cries, and the long hours of silence too, shafts of sunlight falling through the café door, and just the odd hen wandering in. Your arm in mourning black swept back and forth across white sheets, writing poems on my blank mind.

> I am dreaming again: this time
> she's ironing, green valley
> at her back, that scent of damp sheets,
> hot iron, rising on the air.
>
> Last time I dreamt it was winter;
> thick rain was slanting the valley,
> only the muddy slope present
> and the dried vine outside the door.
>
> Maroula wasn't there, that small
> cleft of worry between her eyes;
> she must have been in the cafe.
> The light was on, and men were shouting,
>
> betting over cards again.
> In my dreams she is pale from late
> nights under the white cafe light—
> but now it's a spring afternoon.
>
> This isn't a dream: the sunlight,
> this woman pale over the hot
> ironing, and silence rising
> like a mist from the green valley.

On that last visit, you asked why I didn't bring the boys? My Tall Husband? Affection in your tone for the Good Man you deemed him when you met. You turned down the many offers a woman of your dowry and good repute naturally attracted. I'm sure you would have accepted the schoolmaster, the one who came from Epirus, in a flash. Your face was so open when we all ate together; you laughed, there was a lightness about your being I later realised was gone. He was gentle, generous and polite—not unlike your father, it occurs to me looking back—but he was caught in his own clouds, and then he left. You made that large choice too: not to marry; took Solitude for your own, as a folk song might sing. 'Look at the women around here. Is anyone happy?' you once said. 'Our lives are too hard without love.'

Things all right, you hoped? The cleft between your eyes deepened for a second, divorce the common option now in both our families. Yes, fine, I said, not wanting to get into the complexities of family life, and other skins, and how when there was so much love it seemed blasphemous to long for solitude, which in village Greek translated as loneliness. I suspected you knew loneliness too well, here where life was hard and no one ever understood. You used to love the friends I brought simply for their courtesy, the fact they thanked you for the things you did.

'I brought photos,' I said, and you smiled studying them, told me how handsome they all were.

'And you?' I gestured round. 'This is amazing!' You were pleased I liked it, your face lit up with a momentary glow of pride—but then you sighed, up from some deep crevasse within, like in old times kneading bread, or over the dishpan washing out intestines, or at the well roping the huge tins of water onto the donkey—you had to draw for the café as well as home. It used to alarm me; I'd never heard anyone sigh like that, something must be wrong—I'd look up expecting bad news. It took a long time to realise that it was Life that was the bad news. 'The same,' you said, just like in letters.

Often I read your letters aloud because the cadence of your voice helped me understand. 'If you ask about me, my life is just the same, over and over, I can't go anywhere, and it's troubles and worries. My father shouts at me now, it hurts, it all goes inside me, every day, and the shop so tiring.' That must have been written when your father was beginning to lose grip, feared what was happening to him. 'I can't write details but you know what a woman faces in a café, all men, so boring... Winter now—Erímanthos has whitened with snow.' Like laundry might whiten if you gave it an extra scrub, down in the gully where there was a pool of water and a rinsing-stream each spring. Or now my hair, and—who knows—yours? The way you used words made things curiously equivalent: winter snow, clean laundry, hair all facets of each other, shaped stones in the same edifice.

'People came over Christmas, first my sister with ten friends, then they left and three cars arrived with fifteen for the noon meal, just think what trouble all those people, trying to manage and the cafe too. I'm ashamed, I just can't, I like guests to come but this year with the worry over my father—and then they say "Why don't you go somewhere?" I don't even go to church. "There's work," I say, "there's so much work." You'll be coming back happy from your Christmas trip to see your mother. It's wonderful to have the holidays with your family, but there should be some facilities and not so much work.' Those many years when I went home for Christmas and the days unrolled in a succession of fine meals and conviviality pass before my eyes again. How my mother experimented in the kitchen and we all praised, truly, the triumph she had just claimed from certain tragedy—how she thrilled to the holiday thrum and buzz, glowing in our love... Gone those structures too, even the house. Would you be shocked at all that's happened? Probably not. Your father gave away the house you saved years for and built in town—when you still hoped to leave—as your sister's dowry. Yet even in her failing state, Mother glows when people visit and she can feel they love her.

'I'm sorry I haven't written for so long,' a letter begins from after your father's death, 'you know how I neglect all correspondence, I hope you won't be offended, you know the work there is, the troubles. An acquaintance came from Athens and stayed almost a month, I was so tired you can't imagine, trying to take care of him, and get through my jobs, and always the café. Then my sisters arrived from Germany, and we had my father's memorial with all kinds of guests and nobody helping at all. It took a week to clean the wheat and pick through the raisins for the *koliva*, for church and the priests, you know we Greeks have customs which seem strange to you.' I remember eating koliva, *that God might pardon us our sins, numerous as these grains of wheat,* and wondered if Maroula's recipe included pomegranate pips, blanched almonds, cinnamon, anise seeds and shreds of parsley. I'd never tasted anything so delicious—

and the service I was at was to remember the dead: my pleasure, my greed felt surreptitious, embarrassed.

'I hope you write me sooner than I wrote you, for me it's all problems and troubles and work to face in my life, I think you understand, I don't know why I never have any joy like a normal human being, I can't understand why I have no culture, no education, why I always find myself with the same fate of never having any joy. With that I end, you have greetings from everyone, I kiss you with much love and pain. Maroula.'

The usual ending and the words still feel like stones. I put the letter down very gently. Images from long ago flash through my mind. A goat sleeping under the olive tree cut down to make space for the new café. Children pelting each other with green plums, and how angrily Maroula's gentle uncle shouted. People rushing out to look when a car limped up the rough track past the village. A woman dying wool in a huge cauldron and hanging the red skeins across a thorn-brake to dry.

Maroula's father wandering down the road in the moonlight.

I pick up my pen and try to hear the familiar cadences, and the words come.

'Dear Maroula,

I'm sorry I haven't written for so long. I don't think you will be offended. I hope you are well. We are fine, and the boys have grown up—of course.'

(I pause a moment wondering if there is a recent photo.)

'We should be freer now but there's my mother. She has lost her memory and needs a lot of care. You know how tiring that is…'

Doreen King

Somewhere

Everyone knows this place—
full of rooms with no curtains
bare bulbs
and grubby rugs:

in one
   a man with a black eye
sleeps like something electrical
    on standby

in another
a woman still searches
for a full purse that was stolen
     or accidentally
put out with yesterday's paper

others have booked in
having come to forget;
nothing is hidden

Anne Caldwell

Walk in the Park

I'm kept in a box. I blink.
Smell hot plastic. Stretch out my hand
to watch a pattern of light redden.
I'm a glow-in-the-dark; half-fish
with slithery lungs in a ribcage supple as a slipper.
My skull's pointed, yet to harden.
My hold on life is lax.
Mother's face rises like a full moon
and her eyes cloud over with green.
I've lost her metronome heartbeat.
I've no idea of the comfort of her milk-tipped
nipple, nor the crook of her arm,
nor the rhythm of a walk in the park
with sycamore leaves to soften the sun's stare.

Pregnancy Late in Life

Our house is a hayloft flooded with delight.
It streams through oak panels
and the afternoon throws its arms wide open.
My breasts smell sweet with pollen.
I'm your vase crammed tight with tulips,
life's as spiced as gingerbread.

My body's a meadow nodding with cowslip,
my stems are wet with sap. I mushroom
with content as you stroke
the pencil-line down to my pubic bone,
trace my belly's fishbone-patterns,
then brush my hair—glossy as an otter-pelt.

Let my poor spine rest against your chest,
bring me green tea and oakcakes,
for I am all at sea.
I'm rudderless—your wife,
who writes her lists at daybreak
and checks the locks last thing at night.

Incubating Twins

She strokes their stomachs with her forefinger.
Tomorrow, or the next day,
their small sarcophagi will be opened forever.
She will hold their wee bodies to the sun,
breathe their scent, like freshly cut hay.

Breast-milk stains her blue silk gown.
Robert screams when she has to go home.
She carries his cry like a wren in her pocket,
feels the sharp yellow beak of it.
Throughout the night she sings to them
across the streets of Lewisham.

You Can Say What You Like to the Dead

but talking to the living
is a shout down a mobile as you enter a tunnel.
You need courage and a clear signal.

Resist the urge to redefine
a half-heard message that crackles with love
then fizzles as the world goes black.

I've always been the kind of woman
who wants to end other peoples' phrases,
to second guess. I know it's a bad habit.

Don't text me—it's too brief,
like being offered
one red Smartie from a tube.

We all need tracks to each other,
the criss-cross of an island-hopping ferry
or we end up strange: like the duck-billed platypus—

all fur and flippers—or Galapagos dragons
left to spit salt water in their own
dead end in the Mid-Pacific.

So ring me often. Let me wallow in the cadence
of your voice. Let me download my day's
inconsequence: the plumber who never showed up,

the lack of fat cheques on the doormat,
the orchid in bloom by my bed and the sight of a hare
bursting from its scrape like a cry for help.

Bolton Abbey

Alice de Rumilly founded the abbey in grief after her son drowned.

My unborn daughter's at the edge of things—
wrapped in spider-silk before the abbey stirs,

or curled in the belly of a Wharfedale sheep
safe in the hollow of a hawthorn hedge.

She's crying from another mother's pram
like the last blue-tit about to fledge,

or pouched to her father's chest
as he strides across the stepping stones.

The new-mown smell of her lingers
in the pillow pressed to my swollen breasts.

She swims towards me, arms outstretched,
through the The Strid's deadly turbulence.

Someone Dancing
Huw Lawrence

I'd go through her wardrobe in the night with a silent howl. Afterwards, around dawn, I would pick at whatever I found in the fridge

I lost weight. I missed work.

By the time my neighbour called and noticed the photographs on the kitchen table I had a series of collages made of Melanie's cut up clothes.

Gary looked at the photographs and said: 'Good God! What is she going to say? She's bound to come back for her things.'

'Maybe she's already saying it.'

'What do you mean?'

'Either I'm going nuts, or she came out of the front gate right before my eyes and raced off in a car. If it really was her.'

'When?' asked Gary.

'Monday. I came home from work, sick. I had a temperature, though. I wasn't feeling myself. Maybe it was someone that just looked like her. Still, there was nothing posted through the letterbox or anything...'

Gary pointed at the table. 'Were any of those in the making?'

'The one made out of the blue dress with the face cut from the photograph. It was on the bedroom floor.'

'Hell, that doesn't look like a cheap dress. Anything gone from the house?'

'That's just it, nothing.'

'Ring her up and find out.'

'She won't talk to me. I always talk to the kids. I don't want to talk to them about this.'

'Ask her parents.'

'Jesus, I'd rather not.'

It was the second time Melanie had left me. The first time her parents had offered me some vivid descriptions of myself.

'Didn't you call out to her?'

'I was frozen with surprise, and she was so intent on getting to her car. Before I could blink she was just a woman with short blond hair driving off.'

'What kind of car?'

'Small, silver.'

'What have her parents got?'

'A silver Fiesta. But so what?'

'Yeah, right. You're sure nothing is gone? I mean, otherwise, why would she come?'

'I went through everything.' I shook my head. 'I started to think I was going crazy. I was sure it was her. I sniffed for perfume. I even listened to the bathroom cistern in case she'd had a pee because she's always needing one. I checked if the kettle was hot. I examined the carpets for heel marks. I checked the cheese she likes in the fridge. I stared at photographs and ornaments in case something had moved.' I placed my fingers on my forehead to calm my nerves. I pointed at the photograph. 'What would she think if she went into the bedroom and saw that? But I don't even know if she was here.' I ran my fingers through my hair.

My skinny neighbour was giving me a look. He had pointy ears and sparse hair that curled flat on his head, same colour as his skin, and he had this strange habit of standing stock-still. You could put him in Natasha's Gallery with a plaque: 'Gary the Martian'. Jesus, I thought, *he* is giving *me* a funny look?

Anyway, what happened came about because of him.

He talked to Max Anthony, his boss at work, and next day Natasha Anthony called round. She'd opened her gallery a few years ago. She had already sold five of my pictures. I told her there was only the one I could show her, the others being fragments in a trunk. It was the last one. Sapped of energy, I'd been stepping round it for two weeks. It looked alive compared to how I felt, portraying Melanie in a leap, in her hand a tambourine of purple silk with silver bells. They were not likenesses, of course, those collages of fabric, but somehow they came close and being made of her clothes they were more real to me than representations in paint. Finally beyond the reach of crazy sorrow I could hardly remember what the experience had been like, and didn't want to.

Natasha looked at the one on the bedroom floor. She said it needed a dark velvet background. We went down to the kitchen where she studied the photographs with a mug of tea and asked if I could re-create the originals from them. I said that was the whole idea. She was tall with dyed black hair and a haughty manner and didn't look right drinking tea from a mug with a penguin on it.

She looked up from the photographs, apologised if she was

being insensitive and asked what the inspiration had been, since they didn't seem to convey heartbreak or separation. I said I wasn't sure but that it seemed to me like an otherness that I forgot, that my eyes had closed to, meaning my Melanie. I said I realised this wasn't very clear but that it wasn't clear to me either. She put her head to one side and nodded encouragingly as if I were a toddler. I wasn't sure I liked her. I offered her more tea.

She asked could she come back with the velvet and some glue. She said she thought the others seemed more powerful, judging by the photographs, but preferred to start with what she could assess of the real thing. I would have to arrange the pieces on to the velvet. She produced a tape measure from her bag and we went back upstairs to take measurements.

She came next evening with a ginger-haired guy with glasses who framed the pieces that I glued to the velvet. Then he gave me a bill for thirty-five quid.

When I visited the gallery some days later Melanie sported a price tag of £400 and a 'Sold' sign.

It brings a certain feeling, selling pictures you're attached to, even of a pet or just a view. You are pleased to think of them in other people's homes and to know that they wanted them enough to pay for them. But your wife, just after she's left you?

'It's only an image,' Natasha reassured, 'an invention of yours.'

Well, hell, yes, but what are any of us to someone else? And those images were more alive to me than Melanie herself, who wouldn't talk to me.

Natasha asked me for another. Then another.

They sold.

I reasoned with myself. You create in order to offer your creations to others, and the flipside would be a trunk full of dancing Melanies all in fragments and never to be seen.

I forgot to mention, in all of them she was dancing.

Natasha's gallery had two rooms and a basement that was usually reserved for sculptures. After selling five pictures in less than two weeks, Natasha borrowed them back, advertised, and gave the whole gallery over to an exhibition with wine and refreshments on the opening day. She opened with prices at £950 for the larger pictures. The local rag made a splash and Natasha got the exhibition into other papers and magazines.

People wanted to talk to me, including the proprietor of another gallery. Critics talked of breakaway, flight, pursuit, the surprising urgency conveyed by scraps of cloth, and how extraordinary it was that she was recognisably the same person in every picture.

Every single one got sold.

I did a short TV interview. I wasn't good at this. The interviewer said the pictures didn't look planned, and I said they weren't. She said the images seemed to proclaim freedom and asked if I'd had that in mind? I said, yes. She asked what lay behind them and I said that I was still wondering that. The images were so un-controversially loved, she said, that one couldn't help but wonder about their content. Were they about separation? I said they were just Melanie without me.

After that Natasha set about teaching me art-speak. 'A bit of cred. This way you'll always have something to say even when you haven't. Harmless, Greg. Doesn't affect the pictures. Think of the sales.'

Despite my short replies at the interview she said it hadn't gone as badly as it might have because I had sounded sincere. She said everything boded well for the next exhibition.

I said I didn't think there'd be one. I didn't have an idea in my head.

She laughed and said I would.

I had never thought to meet with such success or to earn so much in so short a time or become popular with people who didn't know me. I began to think about my lucky stars and the rest of my life.

Those who couldn't afford an original Melanie bought photographic prints that Natasha commissioned. She kept the exhibition open for several days after the originals had sold.

I puzzled over what made these images of Melanie so desirable.

It was an unanswerable question, but one that obsessed me, since those graceful leaps were carrying my wife away from me. What were they concealing that gave them such energy?

It was obvious when you thought about it that it was the spaces between the fragments that produced the energy holding together the leaping image. But what was it, bursting forth? What had lain behind my scissors and Stanley Knife? I could remember virtually nothing of their creation and now felt I'd even be willing to go through it again if it would answer the mystery of what touched folk enough to part them from large sums of money.

Whatever was so appealing about those nineteen images, showing Melanie's long neck angling away, her head at a determined tilt, whatever was hidden in there that made people want it, I hoped that Melanie herself had seen it. I hoped that whatever all those others saw in those images had been visible to her, too. I hoped she might even tell me what it was. I hoped it had something to do with love. I knew she had visited the exhibition, calling at a time when she knew I'd be at work. Natasha had taken her aside to tell her I was a stricken man, a hurt and therefore changed and better man. Natasha was not so bad, bless her. But it had made no difference to hard-hearted Melanie.

'Been here before, Natasha,' was her reply. 'You don't know him.'

What did Melanie see in the gallery?

If she had been in the house that time, assuming she really was there, would it still matter what she might have thought at seeing pieces of her slashed dress on the bedroom floor? Surely a gallery alters perception. Could two halves of a dead cow take the Turner Prize in an abattoir? And my images were not lifeless, like Hurst's. Might not all those fleeing Melanies in the gallery open her eyes to the beauty of sorrowing love? Melanie could not have walked in there with an open heart like everyone else, I realised, but surely she must have seen something of what those others saw. She expressed no opinion to Natasha. She took note of the prices and talked to Natasha about the sales. When she finally did start talking to me, those were the only things she would discuss. She admitted she had been in the house that day saying she had no sooner arrived than she spotted me through the bedroom window and left.

'Why?'

She would not discuss it.

'You must do more to support the children,' she said, and this was the only discussion she was prepared to have.

'You've cashed my cheques. They were almost all that's left after paying the mortgage and the bills. How much more can I give you?'

'You're making a lot of money out of this.'

'They all sold very suddenly. Natasha hasn't paid me yet. Anything, though. You can have anything. Is there any chance at all you'll come back?'

'None.'

'Tell me what you thought of the exhibition.'

But I couldn't get her to talk about the pictures.

Nothing could get her to discuss the much loved dance of her existence, liberated by me in cruel nights of raging, Melanie suddenly free, leaping into morning light.

'Why are you depriving the kids of a father?'

'It's over, Greg.'

'They're my kids, too.'

'You can see them whenever you like. But please provide more till I start work. It's not enough.'

'You know what I earn, and what the bills are. I'm giving you all I've got.'

'I'm still looking for a suitable flat, and then I'll get work. Till then I need some of the money you've made.'

'All right. You'll get it. But tell me what you think of the pictures. It might help me understand what happened to us.'

She made no reply and soon the pictures became as taboo a topic as our reunion, till finally the two somehow merged.

What had she who knew me so well seen in those pictures?

She wouldn't say.

In the small hours, with scissors and Stanley knife to hand, I selected a garment from her wardrobe. Crouching over what Melanie had worn next to her skin, and closing my eyes, I invited again the spirit that had possessed me in those nights of creative frenzy. I didn't hope for new images, only recollection, but I found that the slightest brush of it made me shy away, driven like a scared shaman back into the hut of his senses.

The experiment, however, did produce a result.

I eventually thought to take again the ruined blue dress and the photograph of the image that had come from it, the one Melanie had seen on the floor, the last one made and the first Natasha had sold. 'Controlled' and 'weak' compared to the others, the critics had said of it, and I knew why. Hampered by a re-gathering of normality, sanity and reason now resisting the extremities of lunatic grief, I had been able to complete this last image only by defying the increasing consciousness of what I was doing. This image, not so blindly made, was more within

107

the reach of memory. Seeking to relive that struggle between unreason and reason, I held to my face the silky dress, symbol of my longing, knife and scissors ready. And suddenly there came upon me such a vicious, satanic vestige of violent glee that I snapped out of it to find myself trembling. I looked at the photograph of the fleeing dancer. The filigree bells of her tambourine seemed to tremble too.

I took from the trunk a photograph that had once stood on the dressing table, the one from which I had removed Melanie's features, and as I looked from the faceless photograph to the face that was now part of that other, fleeing Melanie, I saw love's power residing not in any strength of its own but in another's freedom to reject it, and realising this, and how I had never sought to avoid it happening, I heard again my destroyed love howl its silent howl, emptiness tightening like a drumskin round my life.

Maria Grech Ganado

Portion

Hardly a life for vision—
a dispersion of faculties
a division of mind often unclear.
I've journeyed only inside walls
not always there, or here.

How many skeins left to work through
though the pattern grows more complicated
as we grow older—how narrow the space
we huddle in, as we unravel
patches left to work through.

I might consider a labyrinth or Arachne
taking up mortal arms against Athena
too daring in her knowledge
of the gods' exploits to bear the weight
of a god's consciousness.

But I think of a snail making its way
under its home—making its way
through the tall grass, leaving behind
a thread—perhaps like those I weave
my own Byzantium with, not with songs,
securing my own body to my island home

sliding slowly hiding in shells
listening to echoes of travelling men.

Tapping

There are some persons we cannot place
inside the warp we tend to make of time—
we don't repeat them
like gossip sifting into the woof of days,
we move them straight into a place inside

so that when doors lock and windows
are grown over by branches of family,
when imagination fails and we seem to forget
there can be other ways of tapping life,
there's this air bubble stopping the flow
waiting suspended in its own space,
until the vacuum can be broken through—

then please forgive me if I neglected you
and can't remember the person I once was—
free the bubble, let it reflect someone
you say that you knew well
but I have to become…

Déjà Vu

Then Gwen walks in, soiled smock
narrowing to her neck and hair scraped high
so that, since Botticelli's dead,
you're tempted to sign 'Creator'
on her appearance —

unconscious, real, fresh

and comments start in the kitchen
where we've come to grab something to eat,
how Gwen looked in the rain the night before
with her umbrella, a Merchant Ivory image —
I wasn't there but somewhere the strains begin:
Les Parapluies De Cherbourg watched at the Arts,
the bicycle stretch to Girton, red brick, green turf,
squirrels in trees, as here,
no husband, no children, no grandchild
and Gwen herself as yet unborn,
unlikely to walk in.

Christopher Simons

Ghost Crab

Consider the whale:
he's nothing to me,
so much more nothing
than I to him.

By the time you decide
to approach my design
I'm gone.

I dig out my house
with a spray of sand-pearls:
the beaded fan
of my negative space.

You couldn't guess
what I do in here,
hiding in the armoire
of my quartz armour.

Like you I look
everywhere but up.
I wait for the night tide
to breathe. I can wait

six months. A year.
I nip my supper
from the dragonfly air.

You could never be me:
no damp inglenook
would content you,
though here you could hold

a grain of sand

or a smooth scrap of glass
in your claws like a jewel. As I do,
each eye a loupe.

The setting sun
may be a gem,
but I'm the setting
of your lost ring.

The Choosing
Karen Buckley

The keepers are marching behind me down the drive, shouting in unison into megaphones, 'The panther is coming.'

I step aside. Gravel flicks up at my shins as they stomp past. A man and a woman, muscular and tanned, in identical green shorts, polo shirts and black boots.

'Make your way to the enclosure,' they announce, flinging their left arms out to signal the long, empty cage that runs parallel to the drive.

On the green at the zoo's centre, families are getting up from the grass, folding travelling rugs, cramming cans, crisp packets and half-eaten sandwiches back into cool boxes. Children are scooped up and carried towards the keepers, who have stopped, separated, and positioned themselves at each end of the enclosure, megaphones still clasped to their faces.

I follow the crowd, making for the nearest entrance. The gap is wide enough to take four or five people, but a dozen or so squeeze through with me. A bald, pot-bellied man with a boy riding his fat, sunburnt neck shoves past me. The man's arm, violet with tattoo snakes, feels sticky against my shoulder. The buckle of the boy's sandal snags my ear.

A middle-aged man in a Panama hat stops in front of the female keeper and starts to ask questions, jabbing a finger at his watch and tottering as he is jostled by the crowd. His face is scarlet. The keeper thrusts out her hand, the white palm almost touching his throat where his shirt is unbuttoned. The man backs away, shaking his head, then flinches as her voice crackles and reverberates inside the metal cone of the megaphone: 'Move along.'

I am pressed to the front of the cage. I grip the cool wire to keep myself steady, and let the others surge in behind me. Children are pushed forward, eased between the adults until they can see. They stick their hands and tongues out through the diamond holes in the mesh that encases us.

The green is empty now, except for scraps of litter. I watch a woman running down the drive from the toilet block, her floral wrap-over skirt flapping open. Then she is in, panting, and dabbing at her forehead with a tissue. The keepers step inside, and, at each end of the enclosure, a steel gate slams down and clanks shut behind them. The man beside me winces. I can almost taste the lager on his breath. The boy is standing between us now, one arm encircling the man's brown, hairy thigh.

The female keeper stamps her feet and turns her back on us to look through the heavy grid of the gate. I notice the yellow emblem embroidered onto the back of her shirt; an elaborate P crowned with a wreath of leaves. Her free arm shoots up and she announces, 'The panther is here.' From the other end of the enclosure her partner's voice booms like an echo. Inside the cage, smells blend. Ice-cream, sweat and deodorant. Pine, dung and hot straw. Mosquitoes flit in and out of the mesh and hover over our heads.

I press my cheek to the wire to see him. He is standing on the brow of the hill at the top of the drive. He starts to walk down towards us, his long, easy strides churning the gravel. As he nears the enclosure there are whispers. Children shuffle backwards, pressing in around my legs. They have realised his size.

I thought he would be black, but he is the sleek blue-grey of a seal. His sides move, hard as the flanks of a racehorse. He prowls in front of us, turning his head, and I see his eyes. The light, flecked green of onyx. The sharp black gashes of the pupils. He paces the length of the enclosure, then spins and runs away from us, gathering speed as he reaches the green. His back paws pound the grass. His front legs whip up under his belly. His body is an arc. Someone takes a photograph.

He stops in the centre of the green, at the base of the wooden lookout tower. The late afternoon sun is caught behind it, sinking over the parklands. I shield my eyes with one hand and watch him draw himself up on his back legs. He stretches out against the tower, clawing at the wood. Then he recoils and leaps, hoisting himself smoothly onto the top. His coat is as grey as slate against the sun.

Beside me the boy gasps, and the fat man puts a hand on his head, fingers covering his scalp like a fat spider. The keepers bend to put down their megaphones, then bring both hands together over their heads in a slow, hard clap. They glare at us, nodding to the beat. The children look at each other, giggling, and turn questioning faces to their parents. The adults start to join in, awkwardly, glancing at each other, and the children copy them, trying to concentrate, biting their lips as they clap.

A mosquito lands on my arm and I feel the nip. I brush it off, looking for the puncture in my skin. Everyone is clapping now. The boy is watching me, breathing out sharply each time his hands come together. The tips of his fingers brush my breast. The noise is painful now. I lift my hands to cover my ears but I can feel the keepers' eyes on me, and I start to clap.

On the tower the panther raises his head and opens his jaw to roar. A deep, rumbling growl that ends like the song of a whale. From the parklands, other sounds come: the screeches of macaques, the cackle of a hyena, something bellowing. In the cage the clapping quickens. The pitch rises. My palms begin to sting.

Then he is down from the tower and bounding back towards us. Our hands clap out his rhythm. He springs onto the mesh and the whole enclosure heaves under his weight. The keepers cut the air with one hand and the clapping stops. He is sprawled in front of me. I am in his shadow. I can see the silver peaks of fur in the fringe that runs down his belly, and the soft white sheath of longer hair around his penis. His smell is hot.

He slithers up the cage, black claws flicking out like blades as he pulls himself over the top. All eyes in the enclosure look up as he paces the mesh that is our roof. In the heavy silence I can hear the puffs of air from his nostrils. The black leathery pads under his feet force down the wire, and, each time he lifts a leg, it clatters back.

Some of the adults kneel on the ground and beckon to their children. They wrap their arms around them, whispering in their ears. A small blonde girl buries her face in her mother's neck. Another sucks her thumb as she tilts her head to watch. The man beside me squats and pulls the boy between his knees. Somewhere a baby cries.

Then the cage judders and buzzes as the panther leaps to the ground. The tattooed man sighs, takes the boy by the shoulders to move him aside, and struggles up from the ground, stretching. Others get up too. The children start to chatter. A woman clutching a toddler under one arm reaches inside a canvas bag and pulls out a packet of biscuits, gnawing at the plastic wrapper to tear it open.

But he is prowling in front of us again, his head swaying as he looks in at us and then away. The keepers pick up their megaphones and hiss, 'Silence. The panther is choosing.'

A woman screams. The boy beside me tucks himself under his father's arm. Children are starting to cry.

The panther has stopped in front of me. His mouth opens in a snarl that I can feel in my stomach. I can see his teeth, the gleam of the fangs, the black gums, slick as snail skin, the thick tongue, and the pink, ridged roof of his mouth. The female keeper stands, one arm out, pointing a finger at my face. I shudder. The crowd presses in around me, and I feel their eyes on my back as I am pushed towards her. I notice her lips drawn back over her teeth, as though in a smile.

The gate cranks open. Behind me the crowd merges again and draws backwards, away from the opening. I stand in the gap, listening to the whoosh of blood in my ears, looking down at my feet, at my bare pink toes and my tiny silver toe ring. Then I feel her cold palm between my shoulder blades pushing me so hard I stumble out. The gate crashes down behind me.

I can hear him coming, his paws padding the dry earth in front of the cage, the rustle of long grass at the corner, the snuffling. I want to crouch down, to bury my head in my arms, but I can not move. I know, from the white dog tooth scar on my shin, about animals sensing fear. I can only wait for the attack, taking deep even breaths to slow my heart. I hear the crowd behind me, murmuring. I imagine them scrambling, pushing each other aside to watch through the gate.

He rounds the corner of the cage. Without turning my head I can see the heavy rise and fall of his haunches. Then he stops to stretch, arching his spine. He is walking away.

'Go,' the female keeper shouts from the other side of the gate.

I turn around and grab hold of the metal with both hands. I try to shake the gate but it does not move. I mouth, 'Please. Please,' but can make no sound. Under the peak of her cap are the blue glassy eyes of a china doll. She shakes her head and repeats, 'Go.'

The panther is moving slowly, back the way he came. I follow. I struggle to breathe. The sweat is trickling between my breasts. At the top of the drive he turns to look back at the cage, and I turn too and look. Families are emerging from both ends, glancing over their shoulders at us. The keepers are herding them towards the exit. The zoo is closing.

He turns in under the pines that border the drive. Far above us a clutch of white cockateels squawks and scatters. The air is cooler here. He leads me through, skirting the clumps of bracken and outcrops of rock, treading the parts that are soft as sponge with green-black moss. Pine needles prick my heels.

We reach the darkest part and I hear the rush of water. Under a pine above the river he stops and turns towards me. I wait for him to spring at me, but he does not move. I feel suddenly dizzy and let myself slide to the ground. I sit, clasping my bare knees, watching him edge down the riverbank, his back legs bent, the muscles of his rump tensed. He laps the water, his tail flicking at the mosquitoes that swarm over his back.

The bite on my arm is itching now. Holding my breath, I inch backwards, my dress snagging on needles, until my shoulder blades are touching the tree trunk. I move my arm to my side and twist the elbow to scratch the bite against the rough bark. Through a gap in the trees I see the sun at its lowest point. Behind me there is a hiss from the bracken.

He backs up the bank, shaking droplets of river water from his chin. Then he lies down on a patch of grey earth, rolls onto his back and writhes, rubbing his nape, swiping the air with his front paws. His tail whips an arc in the dust. I shut my eyes and turn my face to the bark, breathing its scent. I think of him rushing at me. One cuff of his paw bruising my thigh. Bones cracking. I see my flesh tearing in his claws, his teeth piercing the veins.

When I look again, he is washing. The tip of his tongue splays his toes, working between them. The claws protrude and then retract. He licks the black pads until they glisten, then up the inside of each leg. He laps the lighter fur of his chest, his tongue bristling with silver papillae like the spines of a cactus. He shifts his weight to his rump, and with his back legs rigid in the air, curls his tongue around the fur of his penis.

I am cold. I want to rub my arms and legs to keep warm. I imagine I am here for the mating, and I know I will be crushed. I close my eyes and wait. He comes closer. I can smell him. Damp fur, earth and breath like old meat. Tiny puffs of air cool my toes and knees, and I shiver. He is sniffing me, his purr a low, muted growl. Then he begins to nuzzle, the warm black nose buffing my skin, pressing as it slides up my thigh like a thick, warm palm. It moves to my arm and finds the bite. I open my eyes and look at his face as the tip of his tongue soothes the itch, wetting the pink circle of inflamed skin, rasping. I see his pupils, blue as ink in the fading light. He lies down beside me, the tip of his tail brushing my waist as it curls. He rests his head on his front paws and closes his eyes.

I think of crawling away, then running to the exit, but I know the needles will crackle under my knees, and I am suddenly tired. I sit, listening to the night noises, then ease myself down and curl on my side, trying to find warmth in his heat. It is dark now, but close to him I can see the neat rows of whiskers twitching as he breathes and the fur on his nose that darkens where it meets the glossy flesh. I can trace the pattern of scent glands. I want to touch him. He stretches out a paw towards me and lets it rest, heavy against my ribs.

At dawn I am woken by the hum of an engine and a parrot's shriek. I lie still but my heartbeat quickens as his tail flickers, brushing the back of my knee. Then he is asleep again.

A grey jeep appears between the pines and, as it nears us, I see the male keeper in the driving seat and the female, standing in the back, squinting through the sight of a rifle. I watch as her finger squeezes the trigger, and I feel the panther's flank quiver as the dart hits. His paw grows heavier on my chest. His breathing deepens.

The keepers climb out, slamming doors, boots trampling the bracken. They pace around us, checking the scene. Then they squat beside me. The male keeper lifts the panther's paw and lets if fall onto a cushion of moss. They nod to each other, then hold out a hand to me. I let myself be pulled to my feet. They watch as I straighten my dress and pick pine needles from the cotton. Then, one after the other, they step forward, pat me on the shoulder, and say, 'Well done.'

Anna Johnson

Summer in the city

I wake at five to the call of the bread-seller
wheeling his bicycle below my open window.
Women beat their rugs
shouting the morning to their neighbours.

Paper boys sing out for trade
as they thread between the almond trees
and I lie on my island in the
Red River hustle of Ha Noi.

I'm sweating under the net
despite the fan,
unslept, kept up again
by rats at the rice.

Feet finding sandals,
I split the white veils and rise
to use the shower—my body dancing
to be touched its thin tin trickle.

The smell of the tiny white soap
fills the damp tiled room
with night-blooming gardenias.
The air dries me as I dress in local blues.

I eat a mango the right way
putting the green skins back in the fridge.
Feet criss-crossing the white tiles,
I gather my books, hat, keys

preparing to leave the white wood house
and become entirely foreign for another day.

Elke-Hannah Dutton

Heinrich
1941

We hoped that the shadows would hide him

dim landscapes where he walked by night
hen coops where he slept by day.

We gave our savings to secret men
who led the way.

He wasn't a man grown fat on cash
cruel with usury.

He was young, still young
the *Internationale* was on his tongue

Heimat in his heart

At the border armed guards traded with the secret men.

Hannah
1939

Who are these strangers
in white starched aprons
flannels ready
in scrubbed hands?

Bright smiles
stitched onto their faces,
their noses tight
against her leaking smell.

*

Who is this little stateless child
neither Czech nor German
neither Jew nor Gentile
a cuckoo dropped by Quaker folk
into the bosom of England.

Here she will learn to walk and talk
Baa baa black sheep
Humpty Dumpty.
English will be her mother tongue.
It is not her mother's tongue.

Candles

She lights the candles for Sabbath
two in silver candlesticks
one memorial candle in a glass.

Her back is straight. She lights the candles with care.
Father breaks and shares the plaited loaf
with trembling hands
and fills our tiny glasses with sweet wine.

Each remembers silently
her husband, his wife, his children
like the candles, all consumed in fire.

Marina Sanchez

Fossils

My sister brought one back, whole,
but I only find them broken, blurred.
I run my fingers on the moulding
where the light catches.

Ammonites, trilobites and gastropods
remind me of her,
shoe-boxes filled with stones
and fossils till she left home.

The future spirals
from memory,
where she lives,
unearthing wholeness.

Slow

During those few years at a special school,
I didn't have the heart to wake her earlier.

Late again, the Punctuality Police would say,
Rush hour traffic I would invariably lie,
cornered, realising he didn't understand

she takes time to wake up,
have a bath,
put on the uniform,
eat breakfast,
have her hair brushed,
put her shoes on,
her willingness to step out,
variable each day.

But too often, in spite of what I'd learnt,
I gave in, hurried her
against herself, aligning myself
with a bewildering world.

Her birth, her ways, slow.
Nowadays, almost grown up,
she tells me *Slow down.*

We're still waiting for the other.

Bridges

On the train towards your cliff house,
I'm crossing rivers and fields,
sometimes embroidered with seagulls.
With you I try to build
a bridge with each breath
to where you might be, you live
where most have never been.

As a child you kept watching
that clip of the Tacoma bridge,
that doomed suspension ribbon,
providing lessons of oscillation
and resonance, of how not to build,
of what I needed to learn.

So you've grown trusting
my readiness to build out
of nothing, some would say,
though I now know most terrains,
most types of bridges, but still
discovering the set of loads imposed,
the physics of belief.

Exiled Monarchs

I keep hearing their million wings
like pages turning in the wind
or dry tinder catching.

From the denuding forest,
their insistent fluttering grows,
flickering orange dust on lashes.

Their bright hunger among the stumps
guides me, until I find
two satellite pictures:

a few years ago, rare fir trees
were still the winter grounds
for Monarch Butterflies.

Today, the stripped land is a blood stain
around the spine of Mexican mountains.

Cadejo
Cassandra Passarelli

Today I turn fifteen. I won't wash clothes and we'll celebrate my *quinceaños*. Everyone pretends they're happy, but Mama's worried about me and my sisters are jealous. I don't see a reason to rejoice. When girls are fifteen they fall in love, get married and have babies. Men get fed up with the babies and leave for other women who don't have any. But pretty soon they do. Sometimes their old wives pick up with new men and have more babies. Tia Alba didn't. She says one headache is enough for any woman. Since Loco left, she lives with us, sharing Tia Lorenza and Abuelita's room. Tia reckons if men stay they drink: better they go. Perhaps if I didn't have the cub…

The good Cadejo is the creamy colour of ground maize. It helps *trasnachadores* fallen in the street, takes them home. Little by little it wins them over, persuading them to give up drink. The evil Cadejo is a different matter; the colour of black beans, eyes burning like hot coals it's a hound from hell. With matted fur like a tramp's locks, breath like an outhouse after a hot day and tail wiry as Tia Alba's cobweb-brush, Papa says it's a man's best friend but Mama calls it a devil. Tia Alba says it's a dragon with a fiery glance: if it catches your eye it makes you drink just one more glass, just one more. But she's not seen it.

I have. Only Marmeth knows my secret. In Zacualpa they don't listen to girls. They believe my brother, the drunken moonlighter Juan, who saw the good Cadejo. Saved him from a thief, he says, lying in wait, as he returned from a binge: came from nowhere, snarling and barking, tore the seat off the robber's pants. I met the bad one, on my way home from the pool. The insides of its ears were oily and furrowed with green wax. It curled its quivering lips, baring teeth yellow as corn kernels, cracked like mud brick. Its *pipiricha* was the size of a donkey's.

The second time was the night I was sent to find Papa. I was terrified but the baby was sick, Mama couldn't go. I ran faster than a firework flies. Papa was at the first bar, head bent over the table on folded arms, as if praying. The barman shouted at him. When he saw me he straightened up and shook the others' hands in slow motion. We made our way home in silence. I wasn't afraid with Papa there. Which just goes to show. Along the alley, before First Avenida, the Cadejo found me. It dragged me, jaws clenched, into the B'alams' derelict house. It had goat's horns and eyes, mule's ears and a bat's face. Now my belly is swelling with its cub. When I try to sleep it nuzzles my insides. Sometimes its tail wags.

I wash clothes every afternoon. The *pilas* were built the year Abuelita was born. She washed there. So did Mama. Beneath a corrugated tin roof, behind open-arch parapet, bent over smooth, cement walls, scooping clean water with a plastic bowl, I soak them. With the orange and green bobbin of gritty soap I lather up, and grate them across the sink's fluted base. We don't have water at home. And I have seven brothers and sisters, two parents and three grandparents. And two aunts who weave. And four cousins. That means a clothes pile the size of Fuego. Sometimes Olga, Irena or Gabriela help, but mostly they're busy grinding maize or make *tortillas*.

In the morning I go to school. In Abuelita's day there was none. Mama didn't go much because of the Civil War. She saw the army attack our neighbours and kill their three boys in the street. Mama fell in love with a guerrilla. Tia Alba married Loco, a PAC spy. For years the women didn't speak to each other—too dangerous. But after Loco left and Papa almost killed himself with drink they patched up their differences. I'm in the final year of primary – the only girl who can write. Mama won't let me stay on: she needs the extra hands. Letters don't help a girl, she says: we need to know how to make *tortillas*, weave, sell things in the *mercado*. Some men look at the newspapers but Mama says they're full of lies. She reckons reading makes folk sad, like my teacher, Señora Lisayda. Seño's eyes are dead, like her dreams got bruised. I wonder what they were and who battered them. Tia Alba says it's hard to teach forty-five kids, one class in the morning another in the afternoon with no books or pencils. And she's glum because she'll have to marry a fool like the rest of us.

I never leave soap like Irena or stains like Gabriela: it's all in the wrist action. While the others gossip, I dream of my fairy godmother. When she visits me, I'll ask that Mama doesn't have to work so hard and Papa and Juan stop drinking. That Seño Lisayda's dreams heal. That the cub shrivels up in my womb and the Cadejo leaves me alone. If she's feeling generous I'll ask for other things: a glittering ball gown, glass slippers and a bicycle. To eat as much chicken as I like and an ice-cream once in a while. Mama and I went to El Chiche last year to sell chicks and she took me to an ice cream parlour. The split came with three scoops, two cherries in syrup, crushed peanuts, some pineapple, sweet cream and a fan-shaped wafer that melted on my tongue. She had the vanilla scoop and I ate the chocolate and strawberry.

Happiness comes in little moments you can't hold onto. Like spoonfuls of ice cream that melt. I told Marmeth about the split and swore her to secrecy. She said her happiest moment was when her sister outgrew shoes she'd been wanting forever. For a whole year she wore them...till they got too small she gave them to her younger sister. Her dream is to visit the Pacific. Tia Alba told us the sand is black and waves, taller than me, crash onto the beach. Marmeth can't swim she just wants to see it stretching out to other places. I told Marmeth about the cub. She said you can sell babies to *gringas*. Some are used for transplants and others are given to women without children. I don't believe her. They have everything in America, why would they want our babies? She said the women there are beautiful as movie stars but dry as sticks. I asked if she knew a single woman who couldn't have a baby. We could only think of old Jasmin with the wall-eye and twisted hip. Anyway, no one wants a cub.

'Why did you do it?' Marmeth whispered.

'The Cadejo made me.'

In class, yesterday, she sat next to Josefina.

I used to dream of my *quinzeaños*. A girl can ask for anything she wants; clothes, jewellery, shoes, whatever. Mama reminds me it'll be my sisters' soon so I mustn't go crazy. By that she means ask for a bicycle. A bicycle won't do a girl any good, Mama says. In a couple of years I'll be married: what use will a bicycle be then? I could pass it on to Olga, Irene and Gabriela, but they don't care for one. Some day, when they get sent out to get Papa, they'll understand. If I'd have cycled home I might have escape the Cadejo. Since I've been carrying the cub I don't want a bicycle any more. Just a knife.

Papa drank and drank and drank when I was small. He

staggered out of bars, reeling and tottering till he fell down. Anywhere, face in the dirt, knees curled to his chest, waking when the sun was high. I tripped over him once, on my way to school. He lost jobs picking coffee, then cardamom, then collecting rubbish. He drank so much he almost died. I heard Tia Alba telling Tia Elena it would be better if he did. One day when we were planting maize in the yard, Olga found a glass jar buried under the earth. Inside was a photograph of Papa. 'Death' was scrawled in pencil on the back. We went to a shaman to break the spell. He told Papa to stop beating my brother, Juan. Papa slowed down on the floggings. Now he drinks less, Juan drinks more. And the Cadejo bothers me more often. I should have gone to the witchdoctor about the cub, but I'd nothing to pay him with and it's too late. My skirt hardly folds over my belly; Olga's taken to calling me *gorda* lately.

Mama says I'm the best at washing. I rinse and wring clothes tight till they squeak. I used to go to church every Sunday. I'd light a candle on the low table smeared with wax and ask for a bicycle. Jesus and the Blessed Virgin listened from their glass cabinets behind the metal grille. The last time I went the priest said a woman's labour is God's punishment for eating forbidden fruit. Mama shrugged; men say so and she doesn't argue. Tia Alba says it hurts more than anything—but what doesn't kill you makes you stronger. I stopped going to church since I've been carrying the cub. I pray while I wash clothes: for a wider pair of shoes, a looser skirt and a knife.

I shake out the clothes making a snapping noise and smooth the wrinkles with my palms. And overlap them on the line so the wind won't take them. Then I watch them. If something were stolen, Papa would thrash me. I think about Armando. Last week, at Zacualpa's fair, he danced in an embroidered jacket, kerchief and bull mask, pawing and galloping, running at the *conquistadors*. Only the children chuckled. Maybe grown-ups have forgotten how to smile; women know only how to suffer and men how to drink. I wonder if we'll end up like them. As I was laughing the cub began clawing my insides and I sat, hunched over, on the church steps.

On sunny afternoons clothes dry in a couple of hours but in rainy season they take days. The embroidered parts around the *huipils'* neck take the longest. Tia Alba says when she was married men still wore *traje*; the cloth was heavy and they had to take care colours didn't bleed. But today is my *quinceaños* and I'm not washing. Mama's sent me to shower and shampoo my hair but I feel peculiar. Water spilled from inside me this morning and tremors shake my body in waves. Clutching at walls, I hold myself steady, but I'm afraid it's coming. Mama's called me twice, saying hurry up, but I can't move, I'm on my knees trying not to moan. I feel an earthquake inside my body and the cub's fur between my thighs. I scream and pass out.

When I come to, Mama's there and Tia Alba: warming water on the fire. I hear the cub whimper as Tia Elena takes it away. I'm half-carried to my *quinceaños* by Mama and Tia Alba who tell neighbours the bad Cadejo has laid a curse on me. Afterwards, Tia Alba tells me it was born dead. They buried it in the garden. Close to the spot where Olga found the jar. Perhaps my fairy godmother was listening after all.

Matt Riker

Elegy (on entering the house)

Everything seemed
as it always had seemed
till I entered

the mind that had walked
to the welcome already
retreated a step

the stillness around me
soon tempered the echo of smell
wherever I went

in the house
in the garden
memories hosted a silent reception

you were there
you were gone
had gone

near the end of the winter
up north where the nights were still whetted with cold
sharpened enough for your purpose

your plan
in the snow by the steeple
to choose your personal closure

your own way of dying
with a bottle of vodka
to ease the descent

From the Psalms
after Psalm 119:50/141

I am small
this is my comfort:

in the turning of the wheel
that drives the millstone of the world

I am a mote of dust
that may be ground to smaller fractions

but with a thousand million other particles
will slowly make the grinding slower

and at the very end of things
will make the whole machinery

ratchet to a standstill
with a hellish noise and stop

this is my comfort:
I am small

Northern Species
Fiona Thackeray

'The best way, see, is to go with their routine. Roost with them; wait till they bed down. Quiet as a spider, let your nets down over the nesting holes. Then just wait: drink coffee, count the stars.' A toothpick dances between Senhor Mendes' marooned front teeth. 'At daybreak, they gotta get food, right? *Pronto*: into your net. Then, jus' like fishing, haul 'em in. It's a lotta noise, but look around this place: who's gonna hear?'

Dawn is coming, dampening the ground. Senhor Joaquim Mendes feels his bones stiff; Mauro's clothes are crumpled and gritty. The men peer down into the canyon. Opposite, a blue macaw scuffles from a nest-hole in glowing sandstone, and flies east towards the light. Other birds begin to stir, and something twitches Mauro and Joaquim Mendes' net. 'Now!' Uncle and nephew work the net. They have a bird. It screeches murderously. The noise, bowling along the canyon, spreads panic among the emerging roost. Claws tangle, feathers poke through the nylon webbing.

Mauro is surprised by the strength of it. 'Shut up.' he implores. 'Son of a bitch.' Tense with the effort not to snag the swaying load on outcrops, they finally land it at their feet. Breathing hard, admiring its hyacinth plumage, they unhook each tiny knot from the scratching claws. Struggling, gnashing its thick beak, the bird is yet unable to resist four hands cramming it inside a crate, strapping the crate to a bicycle. Joaquim straddles the bike, his broad foot pawing for the pedals. Hurling an empty *cashaça* bottle into the canyon, Mauro perches behind, twisting awkwardly to secure the cargo.

A distant 'chink' echoes as the bottle hits the canyon-floor and the flock's uproar recedes. Mauro and his uncle Joaquim creak and wobble along red powder roads in the creeping light. The bird rebels, batting against its confines. 'How much will it fetch, *Tio*?' Mauro's voice ululates as they bounce over ruts.

'Few thousand at least: they're rare now. Paired up with that other Pretty Polly back at your place, much more.' In the distance, a low-grinding engine toils. 'Tractor.' assures Uncle Joaquim over his shoulder. 'Only farmers here 'bouts.'

Mauro keeps his cool, trying to ignore the sound. 'Who the

hell buys these screechers? Rich gringos?'

'Eventually. Europeans or *Americanos* with more money than sense.' The engine gets louder. A Toyota jeep turns into the track suddenly, 20 yards ahead. The driver, wearing a shirt with epaulettes, leans out. '*Merda.*' Uncle Joaquim stops pedalling.

'Aye aye, gentlemen, what you got there?' The door panel reads, '*POLICIA FLORESTAL*'.

Joaquim smiles hastily, his wizened stubble creasing. 'Just a lame birdie. We… uh…lookin' after 'im.'

The officer jumps down, takes the crate from Mauro's grasp. The macaw screeches; the nets, rolled underneath, spring loose. 'You come out at dawn - with nets – to help *lame* birds?' His lip curls.

Joaquim Mendes' bicycle tracks end right there. Lone Toyota tracks continue on the red road towards town, Mauro and his uncle handcuffed in the rear partition, the hopeful light gone from their eyes. The bird rides in the passenger seat, crooning softly as the sky takes on the colour of ripe corn.

And so the two of them got banged up. Hapless Uncle Joaquim was always in some sort of trouble, but Mauro? She swept more ferociously as her thoughts gathered pace; she'd never realised he was such a dumb ass. Had he forgotten the police raids on TV? The fool. Tried to pacify her about the first macaw with talk of some trucker mate who'd take it to Rio airport, the money that would solve all their debt worries. Just one more trip to get a partner bird, he said, and they'd be laughing. A fool's dream, like all the schemes of destitute Northern farmers. She lay awake nights wondering what to do with five acres of barren red dust and a small baby. She had hidden the first bird - the one they'd got away with - in the cassava-root store, for fear of the police coming searching. The blessed creature shredded the newspaper lining its cage for three days solid: making a nest, clucking like a hen. She heard Mauro had since been bailed. Well if he had, he never came for her.

From the porch, her jaded eye contemplated drought-whipped acres and broken trees, wondering how life would be if she'd been born in the south, or east. Brazil overflowed with natural riches: Amazonia, awash with rain, gold, mahogany; the South East, fat on beef-pasture and coffee estates, soap opera people flouncing around glossy air-conditioned malls. But she belonged to the forgotten Northeast: among ossified farmers watching the sky in vain hope. Upon the ochre expanse of her neighbour's fields, a small child laboured, skinning shrivelled roots with a knife too big for his hands. Sun roasted his back, hot wind glazed his skin and hair with red dust, like a terracotta relic ploughed up after centuries buried. They showed scenes like this whenever the 'Nordeste' was on TV news; people in the South tutted and shook their heads. She vowed her son would not grow up like that: a desiccated little workhorse of sun-baked clay. He'd play in the shade of broad trees; walk to school in gentle rain. All the money Mauro talked of would have got them out—to some place milder, where the sky shed tears of pity on earth now and then.

Her ears were drawn to strange cawing from the outbuildings. The macaw sat blinking among newspaper curls, breast feathers parting to reveal a chalky egg. She stared at it; a pearl nestled in blue velvet. One hundred thousand *reais*, Mauro had bragged, for a pair.

They made a wretched couple: she struggling alone to care for the boy and no rain on the fields for another year; the macaw with only its egg for company in the root-house. Surrounding them, broken-stemmed cassava withered in drunken rows, witness to the sky's spiteful heart. The trucker who was to carry the bird-cargo south never called. Maybe news of Mauro's capture had reached him.

And so she went to town, her son strapped to her back, her head held high as curious neighbours peered in her direction. At the mill-yard, no sign of the broad man who once had helped Mauro bring home a plough-horse. Men loading flour sacks avoided her eyes; they muttered something about a bakery gesturing towards the rusting gate, then turned their powdery backs. The trucker watched her approach, munching buttered bread, his coffee steaming on the counter. He dusted his hand before shaking hers. She asked him would he come to the house.

Driving back across her five sorry acres, the truck's bouncing rhythm over potholes sent her boy to sleep. She went to brew fresh coffee, directing the trucker towards the root-house. Half way to the kitchen she froze: unfamiliar car-tracks printed the dust, and her front door stood ajar. She shivered, hugging her son to her. Her first thought was Mauro. Saucepans and crockery were scattered, chairs upended. From the outbuildings, the trucker yelled. The cage was empty – the bird gone. Her neighbour, approaching her fence chewing a grass stalk, explained the police had paid a visit, half an hour before.

The trucker suddenly remembered commitments elsewhere and mumbled his apologies. Within seconds, he'd revved the engine and shouted goodbye. As the dust settled in his wake, she decanted hot coffee into an empty oilcan, wrapped the can in blankets and reached behind the stove where, that morning before leaving, she'd hidden the macaw's egg, bundled in newspaper. It was still warm as she placed it among snug woollen layers. She set about putting her kitchen back in order, every few hours stopping to boil water for the oilcan, and gently turn the egg. For four weeks, she kept this ritual, holding the egg to the light now and then to glimpse the hopeful dark spot. In the fifth week, the egg grew light and papery; she worried it was wasting away. She sat sorting batches of beans on the tabletop when tiny tap-tapping noises came from the makeshift incubator. The hatchling emerged –ashen-pink, pimply, and frosted with yolk-matted down. Its eyes bulged indigo under milky lids. With a feeble peep, it tipped forward onto its rubbery beak waiting, helpless, for her to do something.

The baby macaw was frail and impossible to please. She mashed endless combinations of corn and palm fruits, banana, and pounded beans, but it trembled and fell over more often than it ate. Foods that it liked on one day seemed not to pass muster on the next; she could ill afford the waste. Somehow, it survived this bald and vulnerable phase and began to open its eyes. Her own baby had to be kept far from the bird - he had not the co-ordination to avoid doing harm in his innocent attempts to make friends.

Over the weeks, she kept the chick carefully hidden. One night, exhausted and jumpy at the thought of the police returning, she wondered if she should have let the egg go cold. The nestling lifted its clownish head with blue feather-tufts poking through, gazing at her with white-rimmed eyes and she quickly repented the thought. When the last waxy feather-casings fell to reveal vivid hyacinth plumage, she felt surging maternal pride. The original cage was inadequate, now that the macaw was fledging and so she let it live free in the root-house. With no cassava harvest to store, she didn't need the space.

She cut some old branches and wedged them into convenient nooks to provide perches. Mauro's blunt old saw kept sticking, and as she cut the last branch, it skipped out of the groove, glancing off her left index finger. The rusty teeth raked a stinging graze; it oozed red. She doubled over, cursing, '*Merda.*' Clamping the hand against her belly, '*Mer-dah.*' The bird cocked its head, observing her. While she examined the damage, clear as the church bell and with great feeling, the macaw opined, '*Merrr-dah.*' She spun around, still pressing on the cut, her mouth agape. The macaw blinked. Its charcoal tongue articulated the curse again. Nonchalantly then, it nibbled a piece of banana, delicately rotated with one claw. And so it was a mixture of mortification and wonder that spurred her to begin language lessons with her fine blue bird. Its first utterance had been a profanity, and if she couldn't quite erase that, she could at least expand its vocabulary to provide some alternatives. The bleeding at last stopped, and she fitted the final perch.

Useful, quotidian things came first to her mind, the points of the compass: *Norte, Sul, Este,* and *Oeste;* the days of the week. Her boy, not ready yet for words, still loved to bounce on her knee as she chanted syllables for the macaw. The bird was an eager student, apparently grateful for some stimulation other than stripping bark from perches. Few repetitions were required before it attempted each word, and the reproduction was comically perfect, boldly reproducing the accent and pitch of her voice. The macaw was reluctant to stop when domestic tasks called its teacher away, and sometimes, when she passed nearby with armfuls of laundry it would squawk words through the ventilation spaces in hope of extra conversation classes.

Mango season was approaching. She stood freckled by the shade of her few remaining trees, appraising the crop. The fat blushing fruits would bring a little income in December, a saving grace. She fetched a ladder and climbed into the canopy. Several fruits loosened and split on the cracked earth below. At close range, she saw black rot distorting the stems, burrowing into the hearts of the fruits. The harvest was shot.

Her gaze, blurred with tears, lifted to the horizon: an angry red line uninterrupted by trees. In the foreground, ranks of cornhusks rattled in their brittle furrows, last year's hopeful sowing. The spiteful sun turned everything to dust, and she knew she was beaten. You could make do for so long but

139

without rain, without money, even love of the land is not enough. Her son began to cry and she climbed down to go to him.

Once more on the road to town: she reached the suburbs before the sun heaved its white malevolence above the buildings. The central district was a lurching mass of heat and people. In a bar near the bus station, dark and besieged with flies, she made enquiries. The barmaid yelled through a vinyl curtain, never taking her eyes off the clouded mirror in which she was fixing her hair, then lazily motioned her head, indicating someone would come. Waiting by the entrance, watching street dogs nose through a torn litter sack, she held down the urge to run that swelled inside her chest. A man waddled from the bowels of the bar, hirsute belly jiggling beneath a misshapen vest. He rubbed his jaw, black with stubble, muttering the details to her. The truck leaves Thursdays, eight sharp, from the filling station out by the rail-track. She slid a banknote wad across the counter towards the barmaid's chipped claret nails. The man handed her a smudged corner of card for a receipt. She could bring two bags, no more.

He nodded at her son, who was peeking over her shoulder. 'The baby going?' A smile brightened his unshaven jowls for a moment, and then was gone, 'So, only one bag.'

While packing for the journey south, she sat briefly to train the macaw: names from her favourite soap operas, Bela Mama Mendes and Eduardo Jobim, even short nursery rhymes. The bird repeated the days of the week with the perfect diction of an elocution student, and its favourite rhyme, *It's raining, it's pouring, the old man is snoring* piped across the yard. At night, she watched her son's chest rise and fall, his innocent babbling, and she cried and cursed at the things that lay ahead for them. Rio de Janeiro would be a little cooler - they'd see rain sometimes but she'd have no fields to sow, she'd exchange her farmhouse for a tin-roofed shack in a hill slum, work as a maid in some fancy apartment. Drugs flowed through those crooked slum-alleys, with violence panting close behind.

Remnants of night huddled around her turquoise house as she locked up. She took a long last look at the peeling walls. The macaw was huffy, squashed back into its old cage, feathers poking through at awkward angles, its fate uncertain; her son was grouchy, having slept badly. She smoothed her hand over the door's worn wood, clenching her jaw to quell the grief coiled in her stomach. As she turned to begin the long trip south, weighed down with a holdall, the bird, her restless boy and a shapeless bale of fears, she prayed that one day she might return, and that the sun meanwhile, if it was the only good it did, might preserve her house. The macaw swung wildly as she picked up the cage, stuttering and scrambling to keep upright. She was losing her patience, losing her hold on the sobs that pressed at her throat. Something landed in her hair. Her first thought was locusts. A plague, years back, had driven her crazy, tangling in her hair. Another, bigger tap on her head; she shook her hair in irritation. But it wasn't quite like locusts. On the ground: other little percussions – and then she stopped, but didn't quite believe it: fat raindrops splotching the dust at her feet. She watched, hypnotised. The rhythm gathered force, and soon she stood among swirling runnels. She turned her face to feel the drops sting her skin: to convince herself it wasn't a dream. Her son began to giggle, sending tickles down her back. Her dress was plastered to her skin and her hair to her scalp. The bird, hunched, fell silent. She took it into the root-house, and they sat listening to the full might of the gathering storm.

From her pocket she pulled out the truck docket - soggy now. She clasped it between her palms, frozen in hesitation. It had cost her almost all she had, and the bus would go without them if they were not there within an hour or two. Outside it was still too dark to judge the clouds. Before she married Mauro, there had been a break like this in the drought. They'd danced barefoot in the mud, and next day green sprouts nosed though parched crusts, leaves and flowers burst from branches that they'd thought dead. Soon brazen red earth was blanketed with green and everyone went out to till and sow in a fever. But there had been other rain showers that came only to tease and mock then pass on through, leaving hopeful seedlings to shrivel. She paced the cramped root-house floor. Rain could leave as suddenly as it came.

The macaw watched, blinking. Suddenly, it spoke, '*Norte*.' She stopped pacing. '*Norte*.' Insisted the macaw, bashing its beak against the cage bars for emphasis. Of all the words it knew, 'North' was all the dumb bird would say now. She looked out at the dawn light, struggling to show itself behind dense, molten clouds. There were days' worth rolling in, she guessed.

The sodden ticket to the south tore easily, and she went to pick up a hoe. Next day as more rain doused the parched northeast, she took a break from sowing. Crossing her blood-red fields she propped the hoe against the root-house wall, pausing to listen to drips chiming from the eaves. Back in the scrub near the canyon where Mauro had trapped the macaw's mother, she released the bell-voiced fledgling who knew the points of the compass so well. Rain ran down her face and her son's and they smiled, watching hyacinth wings spread to fly north, and homewards.

Ian McEwan

Jane Kenyon Known only through her Poems

I think of you stooping (*singing*) on the porch,
the screen door that (*slap*) rattles shut
behind you. The (*hiss of*) light is thin
and (*sings*) un-yellow as winter milk.
A whispering sound like dry gorse (*sings*)
is talking in (*echoes*) the shell of the house,
by the (*hiss of*) liquidambers, through stalks
of hemlock. Summer (*sings*) and autumn (*sings*) and spring
all singing (*turning*) round your point:
the axle (*sings how*) that so wants to touch
(*hiss of*) a road it cannot reach.

Sonnet beginning with a line from Frank O'Hara

Quick! a last poem before I go.
I'll tell the one about the man,
his dog and the boat they have to row
across the lake. Watch his steady stroke plan
their track, tick after tick, the way
those insects do, the ones we call
water measurers. The boat pays
out a wake of twisted cord and all
the time is scrolling further through
the record of its path. The vinyl
surface briefly holds a groove
while the vibrations play at catch—time'll
come when it goes still again, black & flat.
Quick! another and another and another one after that.

Alter

Don't you think
of your double
out in the rain
he's staring through?
Shrugged up
on closed-circuit,
grainy, half-shrouded.
He's outside when you're
in: it's him that
changed the alarm
as you slept. He
uses your mug,
his wet steps
the sound effect
that trails you home,
cloth and bone
golem of code,
his fuzzy tones
on the entry-phone.
It's his palm mark
wounded with drops
on the window,
inside the house,
as you fumble
the lock, it's him,
listen and watch.

As you fumble,
out in the rain
that trails you home,
on closed circuit
wounded with drops,
listen and watch:
the sound effect
of your double,
on the entry-phone,
his wet steps
in. It's him, that
golem of code.
As you slept he
changed the alarm,
uses your mug.
He's outside when you're
inside the house
shrugged up
his fuzzy tones
grainy, half-shrouded
cloth and bone.
It's his palm mark
on the window.
He's staring through
the lock, its him,
don't you think?

Contributors

David Batten's first foray into poetry ended in 2000 when the final draft of a manuscript for a collection he had been working on for some years was stolen. He found it difficult and cold going back to the first draft, so abandoned the project. However he soon realised that poetry (reading and writing) was the best way of gaining some insight into this interaction we call life. He is interested in connections and feels that even far-off events can touch us in ways we may not fully understand.

Annie Bien's first writing commission was from the Soho Theatre Company, London. Poetry publications include: *Quattrocento, Centrifugal Eye, Kaleidowhirl, Mimesis, Horizon Review*. Fiction: *Six Little Things, The Wonderful World of Worders*. Shortlists: Strokestown 2007 International Poetry Competition, Keats-Shelley Prize 2007, Templar Poetry Anthology 2008, nominated Best of the Net 2009.

Sharon Black is originally from Glasgow but now lives in the remote Cévennes mountains of southern France. She runs a holiday retreat offering courses that include creative writing. She has won the *Envoi* prize and has had several poems published. Sushi, dancing and the music of Dar Williams are among her passions.

Douglas Bruton has been writing for years. He has gained recognition in more than seventy writing competitions over the past three years and has been published in many anthologies as well as in *The Eildon Tree* Literary Magazine, *Vestal Review, Transmission, Storyglossia, Ranfurly Review, The Smoking Poet, The Delinquent, Flash Magazine,* and *Blood Orange Review*. He is also a previous winner of the Cinnamon Press Short Story Competition.

Karen Buckley writes short stories and poems. Originally from South Yorkshire, she has lived and worked in various parts of England, Scotland and Wales. She now lives in Nottingham and works as an English teacher and Open University Lecturer in Creative Writing.

Anne Caldwell is the Development Manager for two literature charities, NALD and NAWE, working with literature professionals and writers to help provide training and professional development. Her debut pamphlet, *Slug Language,* was published by Happenstance and her first full length collection, *Talking to the Dead*, will be published by Cinnamon Press in 2011.

Gillian Craig graduated from Edinburgh University in 1999 with a degree in English Language. Since then, she has lived and worked in several countries as an EFL teacher. She currently lives in Hanoi, Vietnam. Her greatest passions are writing, travelling and language. This is her first published piece of poetry.

Sally Douglas lives in Devon. She has had poems and short stories published in small press magazines and anthologies. She does most of her writing in coffee shops or at the dining room table in the middle of the night. Her first collection, *Candling the Eggs*, is forthcoming in early 2011 from Cinnamon Press.

Tricia Durdey lives in Derbyshire with her husband, son, and a retired racing greyhound.
She dances, writes, and teaches Pilates. She is studying for an MA in Writing at Sheffield Hallam University.

Elke-Hannah Dutton
Muhamed Fajkovic was born in 1969, in Bosnia and Herzegovina. He has a BA in Comparative Literature from the University of Copenhagen. He writes short stories, lyrics, movie scripts and is currently working on a novel. He lives in Copenhagen, Denmark

Diana Gittins is an associate lecturer in creative writing for the Open University. She has published a poetry pamphlet, *Dance of the Sheet,* and four works of nonfiction. Her most recent publication was a prose extract in *Tears in the Fence.*

Maria Grech Ganado

Deborah Harvey lives in Bristol. Her poems usually seed themselves while she is out walking, being influenced chiefly by the landscape and stories of her native West Country. She is a single mother to four interesting offspring and a border collie called Ted, and works in a school for deaf children.

Wendy Holborow is a Welsh woman living and working in Corfu, though she spends several months a year in Swansea with her daughter. She has won several prizes for short stories and poetry a lot of which have been published in the UK and internationally. Founder and co-editor of *Poetry Greece* for several years, she now writes a regular page on Greek poetry for an Anglo-Greek magazine. She is working on her first collection of poetry as well as a time-slip novel set in the present time and 19th Century Greece.

Anna Johnson

Marianne Jones comes from Anglesey and lives there with her husband, an environmental campaigner. She has two published books, *Too Blue for Logic* (poetry) and *Ring of Stones* (fiction), both from Cinnamon Press, 2009. She is currently working on a novel and another poetry book.

Will Kemp studied at Cambridge and UEA, then travelled throughout Asia and South America, before working as an environmental planning consultant in Holland, Canada and New Zealand. Since becoming runner-up in the Keats-Shelley Prize 2006, he has had over fifty poems published in various journals, and was twice shortlisted for the Cinnamon Press Poetry Collection Award in 2009.

Doreen King was General Secretary of the British Haiku Society and editor of Time Haiku. She was educated at City University/Royal Holloway and is the recipient of several Arts Council Awards. In 2006, she was given the Kyoto Museum Award for World Peace for her writing. She won the UK section of the International Biken Poetry Contest 2007.

Huw Lawrence was born in Llanelli and taught in London and Manchester before moving to North Wales to ensure his children grew up speaking Welsh. He did a variety of jobs around Blaenau Ffestiniog before gaining a teaching post in Aberystwyth, where he still lives with his wife, Libbie. His stories have won many prizes including a Bridport prize, three Rhys Davies prizes and two previous Cinnamon awards. He has two sons and divides his leisure between writing and fishing.

Ian McEwen returned to writing poetry in 2002 after an interlude working in investment banking: poems have appeared in *Smiths Knoll, The Interpreter's House, Seam* and *Poetry Review*. He has studied science, philosophy and literature, including the completion of a D.Phil. in the philosophy of mathematics. Ian lives in Bedford with his wife and variable numbers of children.

Sue Moules published two poetry collections last year: *In The Green Seascape* (Lapwing) and *Mirror Image* (Headland) with Norma E Jones. She is a founder member of Lampeter Writers' Workshop and chairs Teifi Writers. Elin ap Hywel wrote of her work in Mirror Image, 'her work is delightfully aware of the numinous beyond the everyday.' She has been published in *Poetry Wales, Planet, New Welsh Review, Roundyhouse* and *The Interpreter's House* and a previous Cinnamon anthology *The Ground Beneath her Feet*.

Cassandra Passarelli lives in a rainforest village in Guatemala where she runs a children's library. Born in London, she left home at sixteen to run a bakery, managed a charity for three, sub-edited and wrote theatre reviews. She's travelled widely and studied literature, journalism and creative writing. She won the jam session at the Traverse Theatre's Debut Authors Competition and was shortlisted for RRofihe Trophy, Happenstance, Wells Festival Story Prize, Cadenza, SFWPLA and *Aesthetica* Creative Works competition. She has been published widely and her novella *Greybill* is published by Skrev.

Matt Riker was born in 1972, lived in Switzerland, Sweden and England as a child, and grew up trilingual. Since 1985 he has been living in Biel/Bienne (Switzerland). Matt studied History and English Literature at the University of Berne, where he also began writing poetry. He is currently teaching in Biel/Bienne.

Mary Robinson lives in Cumbria where she works as a literature tutor in adult and continuing education. Her poetry has been published in magazines and anthologies and she has been shortlisted for the Templar Poetry prize. Her first collection, *The Art of Gardening* (Flambard Press) is due out in April 2010.

Marina Sanchez is a published poet and translator. Of Native American/Spanish origins, she was brought up in Europe. She likes dancing, water, mangoes and standing on her head. She abhors liars, bores and winter. One day she would like to grow orchids.

Christopher Simons is Associate Professor of Literature at International Christian University, Tokyo. His poems have appeared in UK publications including the *TLS, the Independent, Oxford Poetry, Magma, the May Anthology,* and *The Wolf.* In 2003-4 he held the Harper-Wood Studentship in Creative Writing at St. John's College, Cambridge. He is a former editor of the Poetry Book Society, London.

Marcus Smith was born in England, raised in the US, has published widely on both side of the Atlantic and Europe. He has received honors from The Pushcart Prize, Ledbury Poetry Festival, Poetry on the Lake, *The Southern Poetry Review*, The Virginia Warbley Competition and The Thomas Hardy Society and was recently a featured reader for *Ambit.* He reviews for *Envoi, Staple* and *Pleiades* in the States. He lives in London with his family.

Janet Swinney was a semi-finalist in the *Guardian* international development journalism competition in 2008. Her fictional writing was first aired on the BBC's 'Northern Drift' produced by Alfred Bradley. She has also been published by Earlyworks Press. She is studying for a certificate in novel-writing at City University, London.

Aisling Tempany is an MA student at Swansea University, studying English. She has lived in Wales since 2003, but originally hails from Ireland. Aisling Tempany previously appeared in Cinnamon Press's anthology *Storm at Galesburg*. She also contributed to *The Voice of Women in Wales*, a collection for International Women's Day.

Fiona Thackeray's work has won prizes in *Scotland on Sunday*, *Woman's Own* and Happenstance competitions, and featured in *The Guardian* newspaper, and on BBC Radio. She has published in translation in Brazil and Poland and is writing her first novel, set in Brazil. This year will see the publication of her short story collection by Pewter Rose Press.

Judith Watts teaches on Creative Writing and Publishing Studies modules at Kingston University. She has read and performed her work at various theatres, and her first—as yet unpublished collection—*Highwire Heels*, takes desire and sexuality as its theme. Judith runs the Poetry Society's Stanza in Twickenham.

Noel Williams is Resident Artist at Sheffield's Bank Street Arts Centre (supported by the Arts Council). His poems have won many prizes and commendations, one being submitted for the Forward prize. He's published in *The North, Orbis, Iota, Envoi* and will be featured poet in *The Coffee House*. Website http://poetryoffthepage.wordpress.com/

Martin Willitts Jr poems will appear in *Storm at Galesburg and other stories* (international anthology). His tenth chapbook is *The Garden of French Horns* (Pudding House Publications, 2008) and his second full length book of poetry is *The Hummingbird* (March Street Press, 2009. He is co-editor of www.hotmetalpress.nert

Margaret Wilmot was born in California but has lived in Sussex for the last many (many) years. Sources of interest and inspiration keep expanding and changing but at present include the connections based on memory, painting and paintings, places and their geography, people's stories.

Cinnamon Press Writing Awards

Cinnamon Press competitions offer writers in different genres excellent publication opportunities. We run each of the competitions twice a year with closing dates of June 30th and November 30th annually.

Poetry Collection Award

The aim of this award is to provide a platform for **new voices** in poetry. The winning author has his/her poetry collection published with Cinnamon Press and receives a prize of £100. We also publish an anthology of the best poems submitted and entry includes a copy of the winners' anthology. We have commissioned several other collections as a result of being short-listed.

Short Story Award

The competition is open to both new and published authors. The first prize for a story between 2,000 and 4,000 words is £100 & publication. Up to ten runners up stories' are also published in the winners' anthology. Entry includes a copy of the winners' anthology.

Novel/Novella Writing Award

The aim of this award is to encourage new authors, enabling debut novelists/novella writers to achieve a first publication in this genre. The winning author has his/her first novel published by Cinnamon Press and receives a prize of £400. The four runners up also receive a full appraisal of their novel. We have also commissioned other novels as a result of short-listing in the competition.

Guidelines for all Genres

Entrants for the novel/novella and poetry categories should not previously have had a novel/novella or full poetry collection published. Short story writers may have had stories, but not a single author collection published.

Entries may be made by post or submitted electronically – send as two email attachments – one with the work and the other with contact details – please ensure you have up to date virus protection and send as a .doc or .docx or .rtf file.

Submit the first ten thousand words of your novel/novella or 10 poems up to 40 lines (unpublished) or story of 2,000-4,000 words (unpublished) in a clear type script, double spaced for prose.

Please mark each sheet with a nom de plume and working title in the header.

Do not put any other identification on the work, but enclose a separate sheet with name, address, email contact & nom de plume and titles of poems/working title.

Deadlines for submissions – 30th June & 30th November annually.

Entry is £16 per entry for all categories (this includes a copy of the winners anthology for the poet and short story categories, worth £8.99)

Please make cheques payable to **'Cinnamon Press'** or you can pay online in a range of currencies using PayPal

Work will not be returned, so please keep a copy.

Send your work to: Cinnamon Press Novel Writing Award, Meirion House, Glan yr afon, Tanygrisiau, Blaenau Ffestiniog, Gwynedd, LL41 3SU or to jan@cinnamonpress.com

Results will be sent to everyone who includes a sae or valid email by October (for June competitions) or March (for November competitions)

Cinnamon Press is Five

During 2010 we have lots of special offers and events to celebrate our 5th birthday, including a free book with every new subscription to *Envoi* poetry journal (and at a discount price of only £12 for three issues); a free appraisal of your work with every booking on a Cinnamon Press writing course and a chance to win a free place on a fantastic writing course in Harlech. You will find details at:
http://www.cinnamonpress.com/birthday.htm
Or subscribe to our email newsletter and keep up with publishing opportunities, events and special offers:
http://www.cinnamonpress.com/newsletter.htm